Emily Harvale lives i
although she would p
Alps...or Canada...or a
months of snow. Emi
much as she loves Chr.
Having worked in the C_, (London) for several
years, Emily returned to her home town of
Hastings where she spends her days writing.
And wondering if it will snow.

You can contact her via her website, Twitter,
Facebook or Instagram.

There is also a Facebook group where fans can
chat with Emily about her books, her writing
day and life in general. Details are on the 'For
You' page of Emily's website.

Author contacts:
www.emilyharvale.com
www.twitter.com/emilyharvale
www.facebook.com/emilyharvalewriter
www.instagram.com/emilyharvale

***

Scan the code above to see all Emily's books on Amazon

Also by this author

The Golf Widows' Club
Sailing Solo
Carole Singer's Christmas
Christmas Wishes
A Slippery Slope
The Perfect Christmas Plan
Be Mine
It Takes Two
Bells and Bows on Mistletoe Row

Lizzie Marshall series:
Highland Fling – book 1
Lizzie Marshall's Wedding – book 2

The Goldebury Bay series:
Ninety Days of Summer – book 1
Ninety Steps to Summerhill – book 2
Ninety Days to Christmas – book 3

The Hideaway Down series:
A Christmas Hideaway – book 1
Catch A Falling Star – book 2
Walking on Sunshine – book 3
Dancing in the Rain – book 4

Hall's Cross series
Deck the Halls – book 1
The Starlight Ball – book 2

Michaelmas Bay series
Christmas Secrets in Snowflake Cove – book 1
Blame it on the Moonlight – book 2

ISBN 978-1-909917-57-6

Published by Crescent Gate Publishing

Print edition published worldwide 2020
E-edition published worldwide 2020

Editor Christina Harkness

Cover design by JR and Emily Harvale

Chasing Moonbeams in Merriment Bay

Emily Harvale

This book is dedicated to my maternal grandmother, Anne Hamilton Reid Blackwell, a woman who believed in looking her best, no matter what life threw at her.
Mary Devon, one of the characters in this book, reminds me of her in some ways.
One of the first things she taught me was that my shoes must always match my handbag.
I was probably four or five at the time and was trying on my mum's high heels, but it's a lesson that stuck with me and I still do it to this day.
Thanks Gran.

Chapter One

Cat Devon opened her eyes and smiled as the aroma of freshly brewed coffee wafted towards her. For a moment she half expected to find herself in her bedroom in Devon Villa and see her mum standing beside the bed, a mug of delicious coffee in one hand and a glass of champagne in the other. Well, it was New Year's Day, after all.

Instead, she sat upright, covering her naked body with the duvet and beamed at the gorgeous man walking towards her, carrying a tray. A shaft of wintry, early morning sunlight tossed speckles of pale gold into his dark, dishevelled hair and danced on his bare, weather-bronzed torso.

'You're here.' Her sigh of relief was audible.

Amias grinned as he placed the tray bearing two mugs of coffee, a bottle of champagne in an ice bucket, two glasses, and a bowl of strawberries, on the bedside table.

'Where did you expect me to be?'

He sat on the bed, leant forward and planted a long, slow kiss on her lips.

Cat sighed with contentment as he eased away.

'I thought I might have dreamt last night. I thought you were Mum, bringing me coffee in Devon Villa.'

He nodded, a sage expression on his handsome face. 'I get that a lot. People are always mistaking me for Mary Devon.'

Cat gave him a playful slap. 'Idiot. Kiss me again. Just so that I'm sure you're real and this isn't all some wonderful dream.'

Amias did as Cat requested, but this time his kiss was deeper and more passionate and Cat returned his kiss, letting the duvet slip from her as he wrapped his arms around her and she pressed her body to his.

By the time they eased apart, the coffee was cold and the ice in the bucket had turned to slush.

'You're real,' Cat said, sighing once again and grinning up at him. 'And not just real. You're sensational!' A slight frown replaced her smile. 'I wish it hadn't taken us so long to tell each other how we felt. We've wasted so much time.'

He nodded, tracing the line of her jaw with his fingers.

'Ditto. On all counts. We're together now. That's all that matters. And we've made up for quite a bit of lost time since last night.'

He threw her a sexy grin and reached for the champagne, popping the cork with one hand and deftly filling the glasses without spilling a drop. Cat sat up, the duvet covering her once more and took the glass from Amias.

'Happy New Year, Cat.' He clinked his glass against hers. 'Here's to the future. *Our* future together.'

Cat smiled. 'To us.' She took a sip and held her glass in the air for another toast. 'And to Kyra. And Mum. And to the Wynters.'

Amias smiled back. 'To Kyra, Mary and the Wynters. And to one, big, happy family.'

'I'll definitely drink to that.' Cat took a few more sips and then looked Amias in the eye, fiddling with the stem of her glass. 'Do you think they will be? Happy, I mean. The Wynters?'

Amias furrowed his brows for just a second before lifting one shoulder in a shrug.

'I honestly don't know. Rafe and Adam are both good guys, but from what Kyra said about the way they reacted on Boxing Day, and taking into account the fact that it's now New Year and they haven't been in touch, I'm not sure what to think. I've been sorely tempted to call them and say, 'Hi'. Just to see if they might mention it. But it's not my place to do so. And once they know that I've been aware of this for years and I haven't said a thing to them about you, we might not be such good friends from here on in.'

'Do you think they'll be angry with you for keeping quiet about it?'

'You weren't happy when you found out I knew. You accused me of lying to you. And I hadn't seen you for the last eighteen years. I've seen them at least once a month or more for each of those eighteen years, so yes. I think they'll probably be cross. They may possibly even feel that I've betrayed our friendship. But I hope I can make them both understand that I really couldn't tell them. It wasn't my secret to tell.' He shrugged again. 'We'll have to wait and see, I suppose. Are you planning to contact them if they don't get in touch with you?'

Cat nodded. 'But not until after Granny Viola's funeral. I know this may sound strange, but I feel as if I want to say goodbye to her – and to the past – before I open that particular door to the future. Does that make sense?'

'Yes, it does. I am surprised that Rafe hasn't been in touch though. At least to ask if I knew. After all, he and Adam did meet Kyra at my house. Perhaps they wanted time to process it, and to speak to their gran and find out the facts, before they talked to anyone else about it. Finding out their dad had an affair and that that affair resulted in a child, who has been kept a secret from them for their entire lives, will obviously have been a massive shock. But Rafe's a really sensible guy, and not one to be fazed by anything. I honestly thought he'd sort of ... I don't know. Take it in his stride.'

'On the other hand, I've known since Boxing Day, and I haven't been in touch with them. It works both ways, I suppose.'

'True. But with your gran passing away, it's understandable. I don't think Rafe and Adam knew Viola. Or your mum. But it's possible that someone has told them about Viola's death. Maybe that's why they haven't contacted you. Perhaps they thought you'd need some time. I haven't seen or heard from anyone at Wynter House since Boxing Day. Perhaps I'll give them a quick call at some stage to wish them a Happy New Year. Or maybe I'll just send a text. Unless they get in touch first.'

Cat's phone rang, as if on cue, and she and Amias exchanged glances and laughed.

'That's probably Kyra.' Cat glanced around the bedroom, tugging at her side of the duvet to keep herself covered as she wriggled towards the edge of the king-size bed. 'Did you see where I put my phone?'

Amias tossed back the duvet and picked up the shirt he'd discarded by the bed last night, grinning as he handed it to her.

'You can put this on if you're feeling shy about walking around the bedroom, naked.

Although I don't know why you would. It's a bit late for that.'

He was right on both counts. She did feel self-conscious about walking around in front of him, completely starkers. And it was ridiculous, given that he'd explored every inch of her naked body several times last night, and again just now. But she was glad of his shirt as she slipped it on.

He clearly had no such qualms. He strode across the room, retrieved her ringing phone from a chair and walked back towards her as she admired him, in all his glory, from the bed.

Cat saw it was Kyra calling, when Amias handed her the phone. 'Hello, sweetheart. Happy New Year.'

'Hi, Mum. And to you. But I'm afraid it hasn't got off to a very good start. Gran caught her heel on a loose floorboard in the larder last night, and she went flying.'

'What? Oh God, Kyra!'

'What's happened?' Amias was clearly concerned as Cat looked up at him.

'Mum's had a fall.'

Kyra instantly reassured her. 'Don't panic, Mum. She's OK. Apart from a few bruises and possibly a twisted ankle.'

'Thank heavens for that. But why didn't you call me last night?'

'She's OK?' Amias asked, and Cat nodded.

'Because I didn't know last night. I only

found out this morning when I went downstairs expecting to see Gran in the kitchen. She wasn't there. So I went to her room and found her in bed.'

'Let me speak to her,' Cat heard Mary demand.

'Gran wants a word.' Kyra sighed as if she expected trouble.

There was a momentary silence before Cat heard Mary's voice again.

'Catherine. There's really no need to panic. I told Kyra not to call you but she insisted. It's nothing to worry about. Annie and Gladys bandaged my ankle last night and helped me up to bed but when I tried to get up this morning, it was still a little painful, so I decided to stay in bed and rest. But I'm fine. Happy New Year, by the way. I hope last night went well.'

'Er. Yes thanks. Happy New Year to you too. But we need to call a doctor, Mum. Or get you to A & E. You may have broken it.'

'On New Year's Day? Are you mad? We'll do no such thing. All I need is rest and I'll be up and about in no time.'

'If you think I'm leaving it there, you're deluded. Especially after losing Granny Viola. I'm not taking any chances, Mum. I'll be there in ten minutes.'

'I'm not going to hospital, Catherine. I mean it. If you must be a nuisance then call the doctor, but I am not going to spend my New

Year's Day in A&E!'

'Mum! Mum?' Cat stared at Amias. 'She's hung up. And she flatly refused to go to the hospital even though she's in pain.'

Amias shook his head. 'I'd like to say I'm surprised. But I'm not. Although I don't blame her for not wanting to go to the hospital, especially today. I expect it's jam-packed with injured revellers from last night. Let's go and see her and then decide what to do.'

'You're coming with me?' Cat grinned in spite of the situation. 'Are you sure that's wise?'

Amias grinned back. 'I think your mum has mellowed towards me over the last few days. And besides, if she's hurt her ankle, she can't exactly kick me out, can she?'

'I wouldn't bet on that. This is Mary Devon we're talking about. And we Devon women are made of strong stuff. Seriously though, I pray to God she really is OK. It's been one thing after another. I thought this year might get off to a better start.'

'I'm sorry about Mary. But I think our year got off to a pretty good start, Cat.' He beamed at her as she grabbed her dress from the back of a chair. 'And it is just her ankle. I'm sure she'll be OK. But let's go and see.'

Chapter Two

Mary seemed to be fine by the time Cat and Amias arrived, other than a bruise on her cheek, and the pain in her ankle. Kyra had made breakfast and Mary was sitting up in bed, dressed in the new, silk pyjamas that Cat and Kyra had bought her, propped up by numerous pillows, tucking into what was left of poached eggs on toast, and obviously enjoying it.

'I told you not to worry,' Mary said, smiling as Cat hurried to her. 'That was delicious. I can't recall the last time I had breakfast in...' Her voice trailed off and the smile slid from her face. 'Oh yes I can. It was when Jeremy was here.'

'You're looking a lot better than I expected.' Cat was keen to change the subject away from that man as quickly as possible. 'I had visions of you lying prostrate, black and blue from head to toe.'

'That's because you let your imagination

run away with you, Catherine. Not a wise thing to do. I'm fine. I told you I was and I am. Although I must look a fright as I haven't brushed my hair, or put my face on. But I sincerely hope we can dismiss this nonsense about dragging me to A&E or of inconveniencing the doctor on the first day of the new year.'

'You look as fabulous as always, Mum, and if that's how your hair looks before you've brushed it, I must start using your shampoo. But I'd still like to be sure you're OK.'

'Why won't you simply take my word for it? Please darling.' Mary's voice softened. 'If I honestly thought I needed to, I'd call the doctor myself. Why don't we agree to see how I feel tomorrow? If the pain hasn't eased a bit by then, we'll rethink the situation.'

Cat hesitated.

'I called Annie, using Gran's phone,' Kyra said. 'She and Gladys weren't overly concerned last night, and she agrees it's probably nothing serious.'

'Suddenly everyone's a doctor?' Amias had been standing at the door but now he walked across to Mary's bed. 'Happy New Year, Mary. Will you let me take a look? I've been trained in first aid, in case of accidents at my water sports centres. I've seen more than a few sprains and breaks over the years.'

Mary looked shocked to see Amias in her

bedroom but she slowly and somewhat unexpectedly smiled at him.

'As you have some experience, I suppose there's no harm in that. But I'm still not going to the hospital, whatever you may say.'

Amias examined Mary's ankle, gently taking her foot in his hands and easing it from left to right and back and forth, watching Mary's expression as he did so.

'If it's painful at all, please say so.'

'It's not. But your hands are cold. Don't you own a pair of gloves? You shouldn't be running around without gloves in this weather.'

A grin twitched at the corners of his mouth and he rubbed his hands together and blew on them.

'It's lovely to think you care, Mary.'

'I don't. It was merely an observation. Well, get on with it then. I want to finish my coffee.'

He used his fingers and thumbs to put pressure on various places and after a moment or two, he agreed with Mary's prognosis.

'It's definitely not broken. I'm pretty sure it's just a sprain. A very mild one. There's very little swelling, which is a good sign. I'd suggest putting an ice pack on your ankle for about fifteen to twenty minutes every couple of hours to see if the swelling goes. A bag of frozen peas will do the job. And you should have your foot raised.' He glanced around and retrieved a couple of cushions from the window seat opposite and slid them beneath her foot. 'There. I'm sure you'll be OK if you rest it for a day or two, but we'll keep an eye on it, just in case.'

Mary raised her brows and darted a look from Amias to Cat and Kyra who had been waiting anxiously a few feet away.

'Two days? But I have things to do. Mother's funeral is less than a week away. I've got to be up and about to make sure that goes smoothly. Surely if I rest today, that'll be enough?'

Cat tutted. 'There's nothing more to be done regarding the funeral, Mum. Everything's arranged. And Kyra and I can deal with anything that might crop up. If you rest, you'll be fine in time for that. Won't she?' Cat shot a worried look at Amias.

He smiled reassuringly as he stepped away from the bed and slid an arm around Cat's waist. 'I'm certain she will.' He grinned at Mary. 'And if you're not, Mary, I'll carry you downstairs and we'll organise a wheelchair for you.'

'A wheelchair? If you think I'm attending my mother's funeral, sitting in a wheelchair, you're greatly mistaken. I'll grudgingly agree to being carried downstairs, if needs be, and to being supported by you and Catherine, either side of me, but I'll be standing up, and I'm not going to entertain any arguments on that score.'

Kyra sighed loudly. 'Let's worry about that if and when we have to. I'll get the frozen peas, Gran. And if you'll tell us where we might find a hammer, assuming Jeremy didn't steal that too, perhaps Amias will be able to secure the loose floorboard you tripped over so that no one else does the same.'

'He had his own hammers,' Mary said, almost spitting out the words. 'It was only my money, jewellery and valuable possessions he was interested in. How could I have been so foolish to think the man loved me?'

Cat poured coffee from the pot on Mary's discarded breakfast tray, and handed Mary the cup.

'Let's not dwell on that right now. It's a new year, Mum, and a new beginning for all of us. Your ankle's not broken. Amias will fix the floorboard, and everything will be as right as rain in no time.'

'Will it? The man I loved was a liar and a thief. My mother has just died. You'll be moving in with Amias, no doubt, and Kyra will be off on her travels before too long. I'll be left alone in this great big house and loose floorboards will be the least of my worries. I'm not sure I'd call that "as right as rain", Catherine. And I don't think I want this coffee.'

'Who said I'd be moving in with Amias?' Cat threw Amias an apologetic look. 'Even if I do, we're only five minutes away. As far as I'm aware, Kyra hasn't made any definite plans about going travelling either, so you don't need to upset yourself over any of this at the moment.'

It was rare for Mary to express such emotion, especially as Amias was there, and Cat was slightly concerned. Mary had definitely mellowed over the last few months, so perhaps this was the new 'normal' for her. Maybe she would be more open about her feelings from now on.

Or perhaps this was the effect her grief was having on her. Grief over losing her mum, and also over being taken for a fool by the man she had fallen in love with. The man who had not only stolen money and valuables from Mary and from Devon Villa, but who had also stolen their Christmas presents – and Mary Devon's love, trust and self-respect.

Yet, to Cat's knowledge, Mary had hardly shed a tear. That was a little worrying. To have so much pain pent up inside probably wasn't healthy.

Kyra smiled affectionately. 'I won't be going anywhere before Easter at the earliest, Gran, so I'll be here to look after you.'

Cat sat on the edge of the bed and took the cup from Mary's shaking hand.

'Are you sure you're OK, Mum? You're not usually one to feel sorry for yourself.'

'Oh, aren't I? There have been several times over the last eighteen years when I've felt extremely sorry for myself, let me tell you, Catherine. And you were the reason for most of them. But you're right. Self-pity does no one any good. I'm not one to curl up and cry. I apologise.' She smoothed down the duvet with her hand. 'Perhaps I'm still a little shaken after my fall last night. I had the strangest dreams and I didn't get much sleep. I'm suddenly rather tired. Would you all mind leaving me for a while, please? I think I need to rest.'

'You sleep, Gran,' Kyra said. 'I'll bring up the bag of frozen peas for your ankle, and in a couple of hours I'll make you a nice cup of tea. But I'll only be downstairs, so call me if you need anything. Your mobile's here on the bedside table.'

'Thank you, my darling girl.' Mary gave her a loving smile.

'I'll be here too.' Cat straightened the duvet and repositioned the pillows so that Mary could sleep comfortably. 'I'll make something lovely for lunch later. Sleep well, Mum.'

'Thank you, darling. Oh, and thank you, Amias. By the way, the hammer should be in the toolbox in the cupboard under the stairs in the main hall. Try not to make too much noise, please. And don't damage the floorboards.

They're Elizabethan oak, you know and I believe they're part of the house that stood here before Devon Villa was built. We've already had one cowboy builder in this house. We certainly don't need another.'

Cat grinned at Amias. Mary was definitely going to be OK.

Chapter Three

Mary was up and about by the following afternoon, in plenty of time to ensure that the final preparations for the funerals for both Viola Devon, and Bailey Mitchell, the love of Viola's life, went smoothly, although she did need a walking stick because her ankle was still a little tender. She used one that had belonged to her mother. She told Cat that, a few years earlier, Viola had fallen on some ice in Channel View Lane and twisted her ankle rather badly. Viola had refused to stay in bed and rest and insisted that Mary buy a walking stick.

'I'm not an old woman,' Viola had said, even though she was ninety-one at the time. 'I'm not letting anyone see me relying on a walking stick but neither am I going to sit in a chair all day, so I'll use one around the house.' She had kept it, 'just in case'.

The walking stick was a bit of a worry for Cat. Not because Mary needed the stick. More because of how Mary might be tempted to use it.

When Mary insisted, two days after her fall, on paying another visit to the funeral parlour to say a last goodbye to her mother, she was the subject of several sympathetic glances, whispered comments, and one or two very direct questions.

It seemed everyone in Merriment Bay was talking about how romantic it was that Bailey had come all the way from Vancouver to visit Viola, and had died in her hospital room within fifteen minutes or so of Viola's passing. They all wanted to hear the story, especially the scandalous bits, and about how Viola had betrayed her own sister. But that wasn't all everyone was talking about. News of Jeremy Stone's scam had also made the rounds. And Mary didn't like scandal – unless it concerned other people.

She made it abundantly clear that she had no time for tittle-tattle. She also made it clear that her love-life, together with Viola and Bailey's romance was no one else's business. She was obviously cross and she hardly said a word as Cat drove her and Kyra back to Devon Villa. But the postman accosting her on the doorstep and asking how she was, appeared to be the final straw.

'Why don't you, and everyone else in this village, just mind your own damn business?'

Mary shrieked, as she waved the walking stick at him. 'Your job is to deliver mail, not spread gossip.'

'Excuse me for breathing,' the man replied, scowling at her. 'I was only asking how you were. Just making polite conversation. No need to bite my bleedin' head off.'

Cat and Kyra had to almost drag Mary inside the house before she beat the poor man over the head with her stick.

'Sorry. Bad day.' Cat smiled apologetically and shut the door as quickly as she could. 'You need to calm down, Mum.'

'I'll make some tea.' Kyra grabbed the pile of sympathy cards and letters from the floor and hurried towards the kitchen, without even taking off her coat.

'Calm down!' Mary continued shrieking as she removed her coat and scarf and tossed them at Cat. 'The entire village is gossiping about me and my mother, and you expect me to calm down?'

'Getting upset about it isn't going to do anyone any good.'

Cat hung up Mary's things and shrugged off her own coat as Mary tutted loudly and hobbled towards the kitchen, banging the stick against the floorboards with every step she took.

'I thought I'd made it clear that I'd rather you didn't discuss Mother and Bailey's romance, or to mention Jeremy Stone with anyone other than close friends and family.'

'We haven't!' Cat hadn't meant to snap as she followed Mary into the kitchen.

'Well then I don't know how that news got out.' Mary waved the walking stick wildly in the air again, this time glaring at Amias, who had come to re-fix the floorboard which had worked its way loose once more. 'But I want to nip it in the bud right away. Have you been telling tales?'

Amias raised his brows. 'You should know that I'm the last person who would discuss someone else's business, Mary,' he said, in a matter-of-fact tone.

'No one heard about it from any of us,' Cat said. 'I haven't told a soul and nor have Kyra or Amias.'

Mary dropped onto a chair at the kitchen table. 'I suppose I should be grateful that details of your relationship to the Wynters isn't public knowledge yet. Goodness knows what I'll have to endure once that little gem gets out, which it will, if you and Kyra have your way. Although I'm sure Olivia will do everything she can to keep it quiet.' Her gaze settled on Kyra, whose cheeks had a soft, crimson blush.

'I told Lucas about Jeremy stealing from us, Gran.' Kyra gave an apologetic smile. 'I'm sorry. But he sort of knew anyway, what with everything going on. And he knew about

Granny Viola and Bailey, of course. And about the Wynters.'

'I can't see Lucas telling anyone,' Amias said. 'He's a good kid.'

Kyra coughed. 'He told his dad. But only because he said his dad might know if there was any action we could take against Jeremy.'

'We'd have to find him first,' Cat said.

Amias shook his head. 'Will Lester wouldn't have told anyone. And nor would Abigail, if Lucas also mentioned it to his mum.'

Kyra's flush deepened. 'I think it might've been Ben and Diana. I saw them wandering around Merriment Bay the other day. They said they were retracing Bailey's steps from the Second World War, or something like that, and that they've been coming over from Eastbourne every day since Bailey died. And when Lucas and I were in the queue at the Perfect Plaice, last Saturday, getting fish and chips, Ben and Diana were in the restaurant section. They seemed to want to discuss Bailey and Viola with anyone who asked. I'm sure I also heard Jeremy's name mentioned.'

Mary tutted loudly. 'Well, that's just perfect, isn't it? I'll have to have a word with the pair of them and put a stop to this.'

Cat had visions of Mary coming to blows with Bailey's grandchildren, and decided she would have to step in to avoid there being any unpleasantness, or anyone being hit with a walking stick.

'I'll give Ben a call, Mum. Leave it with me.'

Amias frowned as if he didn't like the idea of Cat being in contact with Ben, but he quickly smiled and nodded; Cat was relieved to have his blessing.

Seeing Ben again was difficult. More so for Ben than for Cat, judging by his reaction when Cat phoned him to ask if they could meet for coffee and have a chat.

'For just one second,' he said, smiling when they met at The Spitfire Café later that day, 'I hoped you'd called to say you'd changed your mind. That you'd decided it was me you loved, not Amias.'

Cat slowly shook her head, returning his smile. 'I'm sorry, Ben. I really am.'

'It's fine. Let's sit here.' He pointed to a vacant table in the window and ordered two coffees from one of the passing waitresses. 'So what did you want to talk about? The funerals?'

'Not exactly.' Cat stared out across the bay towards the horizon. 'I need to ask a favour.'

She explained the situation as tactfully as she could and Ben agreed not to discuss Jeremy in future, but he politely refused not to talk about Viola's part in his grandfather's life and Cat felt it was wiser not to push the point.

'I'm sorry, Cat,' he said, 'but Viola and Merriment Bay were a big part of his life that Diana and I knew nothing about until your letter arrived. Now Grandfather has gone. You must surely see we need this. Diana more so than me. She took his passing very badly. Retracing his steps and learning about his life here is helping with her grief. I'll refrain from discussing Mary and Jeremy with anyone, and Diana will do the same, I'm sure, but I'm afraid I can't agree to stop discussing Viola.'

Cat watched two ships passing on the horizon, and thought how strange life could be.

'I understand. I hope you're not annoyed that I asked.'

'I don't think I could ever be annoyed with you, Cat.'

But it seemed Diana could. She scowled at Cat as she marched across the café to join them. Ben was clearly as surprised as Cat to see her.

'She must've overheard our phone conversation.' Ben gave Cat a wan smile of apology. 'I told her I had a couple of errands to run and I'd meet up with her later.'

'You've got a nerve,' Diana said, stopping just short of the table. 'I hope you're not messing with my brother's feelings again.'

Ben assured Diana he was fine, and explained, far better than Cat had, the reason why Cat had wanted to meet up. But that only seemed to make Diana worse.

'I'll talk about who I want, when I want. I don't know who you think you are. You've turned our lives upside down and now you think you can snap your fingers and we'll come running and do whatever you say. Well Ben might, because he's still in love with you, God help him. But not me. I rue the day your letter landed on our doormat, but we're here and I'm sure as hell going to find out everything I can about Grandfather's life back then. Nothing you can say or do will stop me. For God's sake, Ben. How can you let this woman wrap you around her little finger? She doesn't give a damn about you. Or me. I don't think she ever did. I'll see you at the museum.'

She turned and stormed off without another word and Cat was tempted to give the woman a whack with Mary's stick – if only she had brought it with her.

Ben looked horrified. 'I'm so sorry about Diana. She's taken it really badly, as I said. It seems to be getting worse instead of better. I'm sure she didn't mean those things. Neither of us bears a grudge. What happened was meant to be. Grandfather was overjoyed to get your letter.'

'It's OK. I understand. Diana's grieving. We all are. This was a mistake. But she's wrong, Ben. I do give a damn about you. And about her. I'm truly sorry for the pain I've caused.'

He reached out and squeezed her hand. 'I don't regret a minute of it, Cat. And I know for a fact that Grandfather didn't. I just wish things could've ended differently. Not just for me, but also for him and Viola. At least they're together now. And I'm happy for you and Amias. Well, perhaps happy is stretching it.' He smiled as he stood up. 'I'm glad for you. I wish you both well. I'd better go and make sure Diana's OK. I'll see you at the funerals.'

Cat watched him go and for one brief moment she too almost wished she hadn't sent that letter. But only for a second. Finding out about Bailey, and about the romance, had somehow made Granny Viola's coma and eventual passing, a little easier to cope with. And it had also helped to bring her and Mary closer.

But Mary wasn't pleased when Cat told her of the outcome of the meeting with Ben and Diana. Mary continued to vent her frustration about the gossip, by nagging the florists, the funeral directors and even Bartholomew Raine, the vicar of St. Mary-in-the-Fields, the bijou church in the centre of Merriment Bay. It had been in the middle of fields when it was built, way back in 1069, and the village had sprung up around it. Sadly, even when the vicarage opposite was rebuilt in 1858, replacing the smaller, much earlier one, no one had considered building a proper road to the church, or to provide a parking area outside. Most people walked up the ancient, pot-holed track which led from Coast Road beneath a stone and thatched roof archway and wound its way through the cemetery to the blackened-oak church door. Finding space for one hearse was always hard enough. Finding space for two hearses and a couple of funeral cars, was a logistical nightmare. Mary had several things to say about that. Not that any of them resolved the situation.

None of Bailey's friends, or Ben's and Diana's were expected to fly thousands of miles for Bailey's funeral, so Bailey would have a fairly simple cremation followed by a Memorial Service back in Canada. But virtually everyone in Merriment Bay would be attending Viola's, more so since the gossip had spread far and wide. Even those who didn't really know Viola wanted to be there, it seemed.

It was arranged that there would be a private service and cremation at the church for Viola and Bailey but that only one hearse at a time should tackle the track. The service would be attended only by family and close friends.

This would be followed a day later by one short service for both Viola and Bailey at the Merriment Bay WWII Museum over which The Reverend Bartholomew Raine would once again preside, and at which anyone who wanted to, could attend. Afterwards, Amias would fly Viola and Bailey's ashes over the museum and do a little lap of the village of Merriment Bay, and Devon Villa, along to Eastbourne Hospital where they died and back again to finally scatter the ashes over the sea. His Spitfire was a rare two-seater, in which he took paying passengers for scenic – and rather expensive – flights along the coast. He asked Mary if she'd like to accompany him on Viola and Bailey's final flight and offered to help her into the passenger seat.

'Are you completely mad?' Mary replied. She didn't bother to elaborate.

'I'm sure Ben would love to go,' Cat tentatively suggested.

And she was right. He jumped at the chance when she called him with the offer. Although on the day, neither Amias nor Ben looked particularly thrilled about spending time together.

On the day of the cremations, it rained heavily, but as the families left the church, the sun appeared through the clouds, and Cat spotted a double rainbow. When she pointed it out to Kyra and Mary, and to Ben and Diana, it was as if Diana saw it as a sign that Bailey was happy and had found his personal, 'pot of gold'.

Kyra added to that by saying, 'It's as if Granny Viola and Bailey are showing us all, one final time, that they're together and they're happy.'

Diana nodded in agreement. She even smiled at Cat. But not for very long.

The weather for the service at the museum the following day was unseasonably warm and bright and sunny – the one completely clear day in a week filled mainly with rain. By the time Amias landed his plane and everyone went to The Hope and Anchor for the funeral reception, Ben and Diana were both smiling and thanking Amias for helping to give Bailey such a wonderful send-off. Diana also said a very brief 'Thank you,' to Cat, although the smile she gave this time, looked as if it took some effort.

Chapter Four

Mary's continued refusal to discuss either Viola and Bailey's relationship, or her own relationship with Jeremy, meant that the gossip began to die down almost as soon as Viola and Bailey's ashes were scattered. Ben and Diana returned to Vancouver the following day, so they were no longer adding fuel to the fire for the gossip-mongers.

By then, the villagers in Merriment Bay had other things to talk about. Like the fact that a retired couple by the name of Grey had just moved down from Surrey into the house next door to Devon Villa, and that the Grey's daughter was taking over The Mane Event and would be moving into the flat above the hairdressing and beauty salon on Coast Road, around the middle of January.

Mary, along with several other people, heard about it from Annie, and also from Gladys, who heard it from her daughter, Lorna, who happened to overhear Natalia and Josh Horton celebrating the completion of the first of the two moves and discussing the second, in their office at Horton and Wells Estate Agents when Lorna popped in to say 'Hello' to Natalia on the very day the Greys moved into Channel View Lane.

'Did your sister tell you that we're about to have new neighbours?' Mary asked Amias, when he and Cat arrived to take her and Kyra out for lunch in one of the posh hotels in Eastbourne as a little treat. 'They're moving in today, in fact.'

He glanced at Mary with a look of mild trepidation.

'I think she may have mentioned it.'

'And it didn't occur to you to *mention it* to me?'

'Er. No. I don't discuss other people's business, Mary. You know that.'

'So if you knew they were serial killers, you wouldn't tell me?'

He gave a burst of laughter, but Mary wasn't smiling.

'Oh Mum,' Cat said, tutting. 'They're hardly likely to be serial killers, are they? And even if they were, they wouldn't tell Natalia or Josh. What's the matter with you? Why on earth would you even think such a thing?'

'I've been having strange dreams lately. Ever since New Year's Eve, in fact, after I tripped on that loose floorboard in the larder. Which reminds me, Amias. It's worked its way loose again. Before we go out for lunch perhaps you could nail it back down. And this time it might be a good idea to do it properly.'

He clenched his jaw before giving her a sardonic smile.

'I don't think you need to worry about serial killers moving in next door, Mary. Not with me here.'

'That's sweet of you, but you're hardly ever here are you? So I can't rely on you to save me, can I?'

Cat was about to point out to Mary that saving her wasn't quite what Amias had in mind, but Mary might not see the funny side of Amias being sorely tempted to murder her himself.

Kyra laughed and shook her head at him, obviously picking up on his true meaning.

'Well I'm here, Gran.'

Mary sighed. 'Yes darling. They'd kill us both, and your mother and Amias would breeze in and find us hacked to pieces in the hall. Well don't just stand there, man. That floorboard won't nail itself down. The traffic to Eastbourne is always bad and our table is booked for noon. I do hate being late.'

Cat, Kyra and Mary went shopping after lunch, and Amias met up with a company keen to pay for its logo to be promoted on some of

Amias' sails and boards, so by the time they all returned to Devon Villa in the early evening, there was no sign of a removal van. Lights blazed from several of the rooms of the modern, angular, architect designed house, and a car was parked in the drive, so the Greys had obviously moved in.

'I'm glad the removal men have gone,' Mary said. 'This road isn't large enough for cars and vans to share.'

'Should we go and say 'Hello' to our new neighbours, Gran?' Kyra asked.

'No darling. There's nothing worse than strangers turning up on one's doorstep and introducing themselves. Especially on the day one moves home. We should let them settle in for a week or two. Unless we bump into them while coming or going.'

Which is exactly how Cat met Dennis Grey approximately one week later. It was very early one morning and they exchanged a few words. Cat was taking photos of the sunrise at the time, for a picture she was painting as a surprise gift for Amias. Dennis waved at her and smiled as he walked towards her on the beach and Cat returned his friendly greeting.

'Good morning,' he said. 'I hope I'm not disturbing you. I've come to admire the sunrise and to breathe in this fresh air. Nothing like a stroll along the beach and a bit of salty air to get a person ready for a hearty breakfast. My wife and I have recently moved down from Surrey. Retiring to the seaside had always been her dream and we loved this place the moment we drove into the village on our first visit. Are you a photographer, or is it merely a hobby?'

'Good morning.' Cat smiled at him. He looked as if he might be around her mum's age, although from a distance, his grey hair and glasses made him look a few years older. 'You're not disturbing me, but I was just about to go. I'm not a photographer. I'm an artist. But it helps to take some photos when I've got a painting in mind. You've made a wise decision to retire to Merriment Bay. It's a wonderful place to live. I hope you'll both be very happy here.'

'Thank you,' he replied. 'I'm fairly sure we will.'

'I don't mean to be rude, but I'm late because I stopped to take photos of this glorious sunrise, so I really must dash. My mum and my daughter are waiting for me. We're going out for the day and we wanted to get an early start.'

She scrunched across the shingles and pebbles, giving him a wave as she left and wondering why she'd just told him so much. But there was something pleasant about him. He had a warm and friendly face.

'Have a lovely day,' he called after her.

'Thank you. The same to you. See you again

soon. Oh, and good luck in your new home.'

She felt a little rude, but she had promised Kyra and Mary that she would be at Devon Villa early so that they could get to Eastbourne and have breakfast before the shops opened. They had all enjoyed their trip the previous week, with Amias, and had decided to make shopping in Eastbourne, a weekly treat. She was spending every night with Amias at his house overlooking the bay but returned to Devon Villa each morning in any event, just to make sure everything was all right, and to spend at least part of the day with Kyra and with Mary.

Amias had mentioned, more than once, that he wanted both Cat and Kyra to move in with him on a permanent basis, so that they could be the family he had dreamt of having, for the last eighteen years or more, but he told Cat he understood that Mary needed at least Kyra to stay with her for now, so that she wouldn't be alone so soon after Viola's death. He even suggested that Mary could move in too. Cat had laughed at that.

'I don't think Mum will ever leave Devon Villa. But thank you for the offer. If I had any doubt about your love for me – which I don't, the fact you'd welcome Mum into your home, shows how crazy you are about me.'

'One thing you'll never have to doubt is how much I love you.' He'd kissed her passionately to prove the point. Which had also made her late.

Cat didn't see Dennis again until several days later. This time she was with Kyra and they were laughing about the fact that Amias had many, many wonderful qualities but that D.I.Y did not appear to be one of them. He was at Devon Villa, trying to re-fix the floorboard in the larder yet again and Mary was asking why it was proving to be such an issue.

'Perhaps you need a longer nail,' Mary suggested, sighing as if she were speaking to a child.

'I've tried that,' Amias said. 'Perhaps you need a new floorboard.'

'They're Elizabethan!'

'They're rotten. At least I think this one is. It needs to come up and be replaced.'

'I can't have you pulling up floorboards willy-nilly just because you seem incapable of hammering in a nail.'

Cat stepped in. 'That's unfair, Mum. And Amias is right. It does look rotten. Bits of it are crumbling in his hands.'

'Then he needs to be more gentle. If only I knew a reputable builder, we'd have had this fixed long before now. Even Jeremy might have done a better job.'

'You're welcome to ask him, Mary,' Amias said, frowning but staying remarkably calm.

'Don't be facetious, young man. I'm sure you're doing the best you can but clearly this sort of thing is not within your skill factor.'

'Nope. Hammering a nail into a board and a joist below requires at least a PhD, and we both know I left school at sixteen. But I'm not a complete idiot and I can assure you that no one, not even the best builder on the planet, could get this board to stay fixed down. There. It'll hold for now but you need to think about replacing it. I can make some calls to the reclamation yards around the county and see if anyone has any Elizabethan oak floorboards that aren't falling apart due to rot or woodworm, if you like.'

'Woodworm? Are you suggesting I have woodworm?'

Amias grinned. 'Not you, Mary. But I think the house might. Or at least the joist supporting this board. I'll make a few calls later and let you know.'

'I'll make some coffee,' Cat said. 'I wonder where Kyra's got to. She said she was only going to be five minutes.' She hoped to change the subject. 'I'm just going to nip outside and see if I can see her.'

'Coward,' Amias mouthed, grinning at Cat as Mary told him that she was perfectly capable of picking up a telephone.

'And when I said these boards are Elizabethan, I meant from the Tudor period. If I leave it to you I'll most likely end up with boards from this Elizabeth's era, not from the first Queen Elizabeth's time.'

Cat laughed and headed outside. She spotted Kyra on the beach opposite and called to her, walking down the steps to wait for her on the front path.

'I'm making coffee, sweetheart.'

Kyra turned and made her way up the beach. 'Is it safe to come back? Has Amias killed Gran yet?'

'Not yet. But it's getting close. She's basically just told him that he's pretty useless in the D.I.Y department, and also not very bright. He's taking it all in his stride and he was still grinning when I came outside.'

Kyra laughed. 'The man's nothing short of a saint. I've given serious thought to strangling Gran once or twice, and she's my flesh and blood. I'm not sure I'd be able to tolerate some of her remarks if we weren't related.'

'Good morning!'

A grey-haired man with glasses, and an attractive woman with an auburn bob were walking towards them. Cat saw it was Dennis Grey. The woman was no doubt his wife.

'Good morning,' Cat replied. 'It's lovely to see you again.'

'I didn't realise we were neighbours,' Dennis said. 'This is my darling wife, Dawn.'

'I'm very pleased to meet you, Dawn. This is my daughter, Kyra. She lives here with my mum. We both do. Although these days I spend most of my nights at my boyfriend's. But you don't need to know that.'

Cat laughed as Kyra raised her brows and gave her a very odd look.

'It's good to meet you both,' Dawn said, beaming at them.

'Lovely to meet you,' Kyra said. 'We were going to pop round to say hello at some stage but Gran thought we should let you get well and truly settled in before we turned up on your doorstep.'

'That's very kind,' Dawn said. 'We're both surprised how smoothly it's all gone and how quickly we've felt at home. We'd lived in our previous house in Surrey for most of our lives. At least since we were married. This is our first – and our last, move. We love it here. We were a bit concerned about moving, especially as our daughter and her husband, and our granddaughter lived close by. But we're delighted now because our younger daughter is moving down here from London and she'll be living just a matter of minutes away.'

'Yes.' Dennis seemed equally thrilled. 'And I was hoping I would see you again. I wonder if we might have a quick word. It actually concerns our daughter, Neva. The one Dawn just mentioned. She's taken over The Mane Event, the salon on Coast Road. I expect you know it. And when I mentioned I'd met an artist on the beach, she was terribly excited.'

A few minutes later, Cat and Kyra rushed back into Devon Villa.

'Amias! Mum! You are never going to believe this.'

'What's happened?' Amias dashed from the kitchen, almost bumping into Cat and Kyra in the doorway. There was a worried expression on his face.

Mary shouted from the kitchen. 'What's wrong? Why are you so excited? Come in here. I'm on the phone on hold.'

Cat slid one arm around Amias and the other around Kyra and they hurried into the kitchen. Cat was almost bursting with the news.

'You remember I told you I bumped into the new neighbour the other day?' She didn't wait for a response. 'I've just seen him again. And met his wife. And you'll never guess in a million years what he's just told us.'

'I assume we're not going to have to guess,' Mary said, sardonically.

Cat was shaking her head and almost jumping up and down with the excitement of it. Kyra was more subdued.

'His daughter – the one who's recently taken over the salon, wants a trompe l'oeil painted on one of the salon walls. She wants it to be of the Roman goddess, Venus rising from the waves in her seashell, with her long locks flowing in a summer's breeze, as she was

39

depicted in Botticelli's famous painting.'

'That's wonderful darling,' Mary said, looking somewhat perplexed. 'I didn't realise you did that sort of thing.'

'I don't. Usually. But he seems really nice and I said I'd have a chat with her. The daughter that is. Her name's Neva. But that's not the exciting part. I haven't got to that because I really can't believe it and I think I'm still trying to take it all in.'

'Just tell them, Mum,' Kyra said, pulling out a chair at the kitchen table. 'Sit down and calm yourself, and just say it.'

Cat sat down but jumped up again. 'I can't sit down. I can't calm down. This is huge! Dennis said his daughter got the idea of having either a Greek or Roman goddess from the statuary she'd seen at Wynter House and then he said that she was dating the owner.' Cat darted a look from Amias to Mary and back to Amias. 'Neva is only dating Rafe Wynter! My half-brother. Isn't that amazing? I was almost biting off their hands to meet her. And this is the best bit. Dennis told us to pop into the salon this morning to have a chat with Neva.' She flopped back onto the chair and let out a long, loud sigh. 'It really is a small world, isn't it?'

Amias furrowed his brows. 'It certainly is.'

Kyra looked from Cat to Mary, tossed her ginger curls over her shoulders and dropped onto the chair next to Cat's.

'I'm obviously missing something,' Mary said, frowning as she hung up the phone. 'Why is the fact that our new neighbour's daughter is dating one of the Wynters such cause for excitement?'

'Don't you see, Mum? It means I can go and talk to Neva and find out all about Rafe and Adam and what's been said about Kyra and me and what hasn't. If Rafe now knows about us, he's bound to have told his girlfriend. Especially as it seems she – and our neighbours, spent the whole of Christmas and New Year at Wynter House.' Now Cat frowned. 'But thinking about it, when we told Dawn and Dennis our names, they didn't react at all. So maybe they don't know about us. Or maybe Neva does but she hasn't told her parents because Rafe has asked her not to. I'm sure Kyra was about to tell them but luckily I managed to stop her.'

Amias sat on the chair to Cat's other side and took her hand in his.

'Rafe told me that he'd fallen in love with someone who had come to Wyntersleap on holiday and that she and her family had been staying at Wynter House after the cottages in the village were flooded and I actually met Neva, briefly, at my house on Boxing Day.' He shook his head as if he didn't comprehend all of this either. 'You're not going to tell Neva about your relationship to Rafe, are you? Not before you speak to Rafe and Adam, surely?'

'No. But if Rafe and Adam have said anything about us, she may say something. And if they haven't, then hopefully she'll tell Rafe that she's met me and Kyra, and then he'll get in contact with us after that. I don't know. I haven't really thought it through. Um. We're going to the salon at 11 this morning. Will you come with us? Just to make sure I don't say anything I shouldn't and really put my foot in it.'

'Of course. If you both want me to.'

Kyra smiled at Amias. 'I think Mum's more concerned that it'll be me who blurts something out. So yes. I think it's a good idea if you come with us.'

Mary coughed. 'And what about me? If you think you're going to meet this Neva, or whatever her name is, and leave me here wondering what's going on and what's being said, you're mistaken. This affects me too, you know.'

'I know, Mum.' Cat reached out a hand to Mary. 'But you've got to remember that you were 'the other woman' as far as Rafe and Adam are concerned. They might not be so happy to meet you.'

'They won't be there, will they? We're going to the salon on Coast Road, not to Wynter House. I told you before, Catherine. Don't ever expect to get an invitation to tea at that house.'

'I think Gran should come too,' Kyra said. 'And besides, we were going to go to Bella Vista for lunch today, weren't we? It's only on the opposite corner and it's open from 10.30 for coffees. If things get a bit awkward, Gran and I can go there and you and Amias can join us later.'

Chapter Five

Cat had walked past The Mane Event several times but she had never really looked at it until now. As the four of them approached the two large picture windows either side of a central glass door, she noticed the windows appeared to front a spacious reception area in which there was a desk, half covered with a dust sheet, shelves for product displays, and what was probably a sofa but was also covered by a sheet and was pushed to one side.

She hesitated for a second. She could see Dennis and his wife Dawn, but she could also see three young women around her own age, any one of whom could be Neva. There were also three other men, all with their backs to the door. Perhaps they were workmen, helping with what looked as if it might be a major refurbishment of the salon. But they didn't look like workmen, somehow.

Kyra pushed open the door and a bell

tinkled overhead.

Cat gasped as the three men turned. She had seen one of the men before. A few months ago. At the early Christmas Market. It was Adam Wynter. Her astonished gaze drifted across to the man standing beside him. That must be Rafe. They looked so alike they were obviously brothers.

Why were the Wynters here? Had Dennis and Dawn known about Cat and Kyra all along? Had they arranged this meeting for reasons other than for Cat and Kyra to meet their daughter?

'Oh God,' Amias whispered, squeezing Cat's hand. 'Rafe and Adam are here. And Gavin. Be brave, Cat. You've got this.'

Cat wanted to run, but she'd been doing that for most of her life. It was time to face the music. Or at least, to face the family she knew so little about.

'Hello, everyone,' Amias said, as they all walked into the salon. 'I hope you don't mind me being here, Rafe and Adam, but Cat wanted me to come. This is Cat Devon, her daughter, Kyra, and Cat's mother, Mary. And there's something you both need to know.'

'Those are the two men from Boxing Day,' Kyra said, pointing at Rafe and Adam.

'Yes,' Rafe said. 'And there's something you need to know as well.'

'Er. Unless I'm very much mistaken,' Neva

said. 'I think they already do.'

'You know?' Cat stared at Rafe and Adam.

Adam nodded. 'We found out on Boxing Day.'

'Assuming you're all talking about the same thing,' Mary Devon said, looking rather awkward.

'That we're your brothers, Catherine.' Rafe held out his hand. 'And your uncles, Kyra. We're both very pleased to meet you. Do you prefer to be called Cat?'

'Oh my God!' Cat said, bursting into tears.

Kyra smiled. 'Don't mind my mum.' She took Rafe's hand and shook it firmly before doing the same to Adam. 'She gets a bit emotional. We're both pleased to meet you. I'm sorry if I was rude on Boxing Day but I had no idea who you were at the time. You see, we didn't know about you either until that same day. It seems both our families kept the secret.'

Cat turned to them and smiled, wiping away her tears with the handkerchief Amias gave her. She took their hands but to her surprise, Rafe pulled her into a hug.

'I'm sorry,' he said, releasing her as quickly. 'I didn't mean to do that. But the excitement of meeting our sister has got the better of me.'

Cat smiled. 'Please don't apologise. I want to do the same.'

She hugged him again before hugging

Adam. Then both men hugged Kyra. Before long, nearly everyone else was in tears as further introductions were made.

'This is my girlfriend, Neva,' Rafe said. 'And her best friend, Jo. This is Hazel, Adam's girlfriend. And this is Gavin, our friend and also the groundskeeper at Wynter House.

'So you know our sister?' Adam asked Amias, looking surprised. 'It's certainly a small world.'

'Smaller than you think. Cat and I are in love. In fact, I've loved her for most of my life.'

He slid an arm around Cat's waist and the other arm around Kyra's shoulders.

'What?' Rafe laughed. 'How? When? Why didn't we know about any of this?'

'I think we all have a lot to discuss,' Amias said. 'And one or two confessions to make. I hope we can all forgive and forget. Life's far too short to do otherwise, as we've recently come to realise.'

'I agree with you on that,' Rafe said. 'We were going to try to contact you, Cat and invite you to Wynter House for tea.'

Cat gave a nervous but excited laugh and looked at Mary.

'Did you hear that, Mum? We've been invited to Wynter House for tea. It seems things are definitely changing.' She smiled at Rafe and Adam. 'Don't worry. That's a little joke between my mum and me. I have so many questions but I think I'm still in a state of shock. This isn't how I imagined meeting you for the first time.'

'Same here,' Adam said.

Rafe grinned. 'When Dennis told us who you were this morning, and that you were coming here, we did consider leaving. But only for a second. It has been too long. There didn't seem much point in waiting any longer.'

'I'm glad it happened this way,' Cat said. 'I asked Amias to come because I was nervous, but the moment we walked in, I felt completely at ease.'

'You burst into tears, Mum,' Kyra said, laughing.

Cat shrugged. 'I seem to do that a lot lately. But they're tears of joy, not sadness.'

'We heard about your grandmother,' Rafe said, with a genuine look of compassion. 'I'm sorry for your loss.'

'Thank you. That was a dreadful shock. We had been estranged for years and I didn't get a chance to say goodbye. But that's another story and one that can wait. I have so much to tell you and so many questions to ask. And I want to hear all about you. I don't know where to start.'

Dawn Grey smiled. 'Let's start by sorting out some chairs and sitting down with a nice cup of tea. And perhaps a slice of cake.'

'That sounds good to me,' Cat said,

returning the smile.

Rafe beamed. 'And to me. After all, we've got to start somewhere. We've got our entire lives so far to catch up with, and our futures in which to do it.'

Chapter Six

It was the first night Cat had spent in her bed in Devon Villa since the one before New Year's Eve and she woke up feeling disorientated. At least for a moment or two. Especially when Amias appeared with two large mugs of coffee.

'Where are we?'

She sat up and laughed, no longer feeling the need to cover her naked body with a duvet, or with anything at all, in front of him. But he was dressed, although his jumper was inside out. He put the mugs on the bedside table, threw off his clothes and climbed back into bed, laughing.

'I felt the same when I woke up. I never thought I'd be in your bed in this house. I couldn't believe it last night when Mary suggested I should stay.'

'I was quite surprised myself. But I think when I said I was going to stay, she felt a little guilty. She knew I was staying for her sake, and for Kyra's of course, after such an emotional day. Not that either of them needed me. I was the only one of us who was an emotional wreck.'

'Not a wreck.' He kissed her cheek. 'But I don't think I've ever seen anyone cry quite so many happy tears, I'll admit. It was a good day though, wasn't it?'

Cat nodded as he handed her one of the mugs of coffee.

'It was a wonderful day. I don't think Kyra and I could've planned a better way to meet our 'new' family, even if we'd spent the next six weeks trying to arrange the perfect scenario. I was a bit shocked when I first saw Rafe and Adam. About one hundred emotions shot through me at the same time. I hope I didn't come across to everyone as a blubbering idiot. More importantly, I hope Rafe and Adam didn't think that.'

'From what they both said to me, I'm pretty sure they thought you were lovely. You and Kyra both. They couldn't stop smiling. They were even kind to Mary. And considering that she was their dad's mistress, I think that shows how special the pair of them are. They even forgave me for keeping the secret. Although Adam did ask if there were any other siblings hidden away that I might know about. He was joking, don't worry.'

Cat let out a small sigh. 'It's going to take

me a little while to get used to this. To having two brothers, I mean. It's so strange and yet it felt so right yesterday. In some ways I felt as if I'd known them all my life. They didn't feel like strangers. It was more like family or friends that I hadn't seen for a long time. Did you notice how they both hesitated when I mentioned Olivia Wynter though? It was almost as if they don't want me to meet her yet.'

'They probably don't. But that's because of how Olivia may possibly react, not about them not wanting to introduce you to her, believe me. Olivia was the one who wanted this secret kept hidden, remember. I got the distinct impression that she isn't best pleased it's all come out in the open. And when Dawn mentioned Olivia's heart attack on Boxing Day, I'm pretty certain it was a result of them finding out about you and Kyra, although they tried to suggest it wasn't.'

Cat sipped her coffee and nodded. 'Yes. Jo also let something slip, but Neva nudged her and gave her a quelling look and Jo tried to backtrack. Basically though, she said that Rafe had, and I'm quoting Jo here, "threatened to throw the old bat out if she didn't change her ways and didn't welcome you and Kyra into the family, as well as Neva". It seems Olivia doesn't like Rafe's girlfriend, either.'

'I don't think Olivia likes anyone. I've only met her a few times over the years, because she seems to avoid company whenever possible, and she's always looked at me as if she'd rather I wasn't a friend of her grandsons. I can remember being told that she was once a beauty, inside and out, but that when her husband Sebastian died, she turned very ugly. She hated the world and everyone in it.'

'It's so sad to think that Love can be the cause of such bitterness. She loves Rafe and Adam though, doesn't she?'

'I'm sure she does. In her own odd way.' He grinned suddenly. 'But let's not talk about Olivia. I love you. Have I told you that today?'

'No.' Cat grinned back. 'And before you say you're going to show me how much, remember Dennis said he'd pop in early this morning to take a look at that floorboard in the larder, so you'll have to wait until tonight.'

Cat deftly slid out of bed, and out of Amias' reach, her coffee mug still clasped in her hands.

Amias pulled a face. 'That bloody floorboard has a lot to answer for. But it's handy that Dennis is a retired builder and that he lives next door.' He threw the duvet off, got out of bed and grabbed her hand, relieving her of her coffee as he led her towards the shower. 'If we shower together we'll save some time. And I can tell you how much I love you while washing your back.'

Cat burst out laughing.

'Was Mum up when you made our coffee?'

Amias shook his head. 'Nope. And Kyra was on her way out to take some photos. She said she'd be back in half an hour.'

'OK. We've got about twenty minutes. But not a second more.'

Thirty minutes later, they walked into the kitchen hand in hand where Kyra was making coffee and Mary was about to show Dennis the loose floorboard.

'Amias has done his best,' Mary was saying as she led Dennis towards the larder, 'but no matter how many times he hammers it down, it just keeps popping up again.'

'Morning everyone,' Cat said, surprised by Dennis' early arrival. It wasn't even 8 yet. 'We didn't know you were here, Dennis.'

'Good morning.' Dennis turned and smiled. 'I bumped into Kyra on the beach and she said you're all early risers, so I could look at the floorboard now. I hope that's OK.'

'Of course.'

Cat sat at the table while Amias went to the sink and rinsed the two mugs he'd brought down with him.

'Put those in the dishwasher,' Kyra said, grinning. 'I've put cups and saucers on the table. Gran wanted to use the good china as we have another guest. I've also put some croissants in the oven, but I can make toast if you'd prefer.'

'Croissants are great, thanks,' Amias said.

'What's the verdict?' Cat called to Dennis after a few minutes.

'I'm afraid the board may need to be replaced, although it might be possible to repair it.'

Amias grinned at Cat as he sat at the table. 'That'll please Mary,' he whispered.

Cat heard what sounded like wood splitting, followed by a shriek from Mary. Cat, Amias and Kyra all dashed to the larder door and peered in.

'What's happened?' Kyra asked.

'I think I've discovered why the floorboard won't stay nailed down,' Dennis said. 'The board has definitely seen better days, there's no doubt about that, but then it is Elizabethan and even such good quality oak boards don't last forever. The joist beneath is virtually non-existent.' He had taken up the floorboard and it was lying to one side of him as he knelt on the remaining boards. 'And this joist is far earlier than the Edwardian period. I'd say this is part of a Georgian, or possibly even a Tudor property that might have been demolished when they built Devon Villa. Actually, I think the joist is the same age as the floorboard. Elizabethan.'

'There was a house here previously,' Mary said. 'Also owned by our family. I can recall Mother showing me the deeds of Devon Villa and some earlier property deeds. So does this mean the joist will also have to be replaced?'

'If you want the floorboards to stay put, and to prevent further damage, I'm afraid it does. It's not a major job though, depending on how far this joist goes and whether the other joists are as bad. But it does mean all the boards will have to come up.' He leant forward and peered down into the gap. 'What is really interesting is that I think this is a cellar.'

'We don't have a cellar,' Mary said. 'It's just the foundation space or whatever it's called.'

Dennis took his phone from his trouser pocket and shone the beam between the remaining boards.

'No. These houses are built on sandstone. It's definitely a cellar. The foundations will be below, and probably fairly shallow. What's more, it looks as if there are things stored down there. I can see a couple of chairs. Oak, unless I'm mistaken, although it's difficult to see from here. And what looks like an oak coffer.'

'A coffin?' Kyra shrieked.

Amias grinned. 'A coffer. It's an old wooden chest.'

'Phew. A chest? What? Like a treasure chest?'

Mary laughed. 'I hardly think there would be a treasure chest hidden beneath Devon Villa, darling.'

'Why not, Gran? You didn't know there was a cellar hidden beneath the house.'

Kyra had a point.

'Why did none of us know there was a cellar?' Cat asked.

'There must be access to it from somewhere,' Dennis said. 'But I don't suppose you want to take up all the tiles in the kitchen to find it. Unless the access was once from here and these boards were taken from another part of the old house, and the cellar sealed up on purpose. The floorboards are nailed close together and there's no trap door or cellar hatch anywhere here, you'll notice. Looking more closely at this floor, I'd say these floorboards are all from the original house, based on their size. Baltic fir or pine was used for most rooms in houses by the Edwardian period, which is when Devon Villa was built, and oak was only used for either main staircases or very grand rooms. So this larder floor was either part of the original house and in what was once a much grander room, or an entrance hall, or as I said just now, these boards were moved from elsewhere. The footprint of both houses might not be the same. The ground floor of the earlier house may have been smaller or larger than the ground floor of this one. This is all rather exciting.'

'Why would someone move a load of floorboards?' Kyra asked.

'More to the point,' Amias said, 'why would anyone leave those chairs and that coffer down there and then board the cellar up?'

Chapter Seven

Obviously, they had to find out the answer to that question. But Cat wasn't sure she could cope with another mystery just yet. Especially as her main priority now was getting to know her brothers and spending time with them.

Yesterday, they had all agreed they would wait a day or two before meeting up again, just to let everything sink in. Rafe had suggested the Devons, and Amias, might like to visit Wynter House, either for morning coffee, afternoon tea, for lunch, or for a tour of the gin distillery he and his friend Sean Small, the owner of the Wyntersleap Inn, had set up, along with a little help from Adam.

'It's only small,' Rafe had said. 'It's in the Old Barn, a little way from the house. But it's worth a look if you like gin.'

'Who doesn't like gin?' Cat didn't, particularly. But she wasn't going to let them know that. And she hadn't had any for years, so perhaps her palate had changed and she would enjoy a glass now. If her brothers owned their own distillery, she was determined to give gin another try. 'But we're happy to come for coffee or tea, or anything really. We'll let you decide and I'll wait to hear from you. It sounds as if you've got your hands full at the moment.' Rafe had already told them there were several villagers staying at Wynter House, due to Wyntersleap village flooding at Christmas.

'It'll take some time for the cottages to dry out,' he had said. 'Although we've finally got the humidifiers going now that the water has receded and River Wynter has returned to close to its usual level. But our guests will remain at Wynter House for several more weeks, I should think.'

Cat hoped it wouldn't be long before she heard from her brothers again. But for now there was this mystery of a possible cellar.

'The boards will have to come up then, I suppose,' Mary was saying. 'Regardless of whether the other joists need any repairs. We have to gain access and see if there's anything in that coffer. I don't think any of us will get any sleep tonight unless we do.'

'I've got a free day,' Amias said.

'Most of my days are free at the moment,' Dennis added. 'Unless Neva wants me to do anything at her salon, that is. But I believe she, Dawn and Jo are going shopping in Eastbourne today to buy a few more things for the salon and the flat, so I can give you a hand if you like.'

Mary hesitated for a moment. 'Will this be expensive?'

'To remove the boards for access?' Dennis shook his head. 'No charge from me. I'll happily take them up in exchange for coffee and croissants. It'll only take about half an hour if Amias and I set to work. We'll need to be careful not to damage the boards and joists if possible but we'll only need to remove about seven or eight to make room for that coffer to come out. We can set up a makeshift pulley hoist, depending on the weight of the thing. And of course, I'd suggest you open it first to see what's inside, if anything.'

Amias laughed. 'Yes. We don't want to try to lift out a coffer full of gold bars, do we?'

'If only,' Mary said. 'Knowing our luck, it's more likely to contain old bricks.'

'Old bricks have value,' Dennis said.

'Hmm.' Mary didn't look convinced.

'I could squeeze down there if you took just a couple more boards up,' Kyra said.

'I'm not sure I'd like that.' Cat shook her head. 'What if there's something ... unpleasant in that thing?'

'Like what?' Kyra laughed. 'Oh, like a body you mean? But Amias said it's a coffer not a coffin.'

'Of course there won't be a body in it.

That's not what I meant. But who knows how long it's been down there? There could be mice running around inside. Or rats.'

'I doubt it,' Amias said. 'But I think Cat's right, Kyra. It might be better if Dennis or I take a look first.'

'Fine. But I want to come down too. I want to see if it's just this bit or if the cellar goes any further under the house. Weren't there smugglers around here from the early 1500s and onwards? There might be all sorts of things down there. Like kegs of brandy, or bolts of silk. Or a secret passage or something.'

Everyone looked at Kyra.

And then the oven beeped and Cat gasped loudly.

'That's the croissants, Mum. Don't panic.'

'I'll have mine cold,' Amias said, wrapping his arms around Cat in a reassuring hug. 'The sooner we get these boards up, the sooner we can stop wondering about the coffer. And we'll be able to get the boards back down, even if it is just a temporary measure.'

'I agree,' Dennis said. 'I'm keen to get down there and take a look. Nothing excites me more than old houses and little discoveries like this. If only my son-in-law Nigel were here. He'd be in his element. But it's a good thing my granddaughter Sasha isn't. She'd be convinced that coffer contained a body and that some fiendish crime had been committed.'

'How old is she?' Cat asked, after a few deep breaths.

Why was she feeling so jumpy? So apprehensive? The coffer was probably empty. That made her smile. Many people had empty coffers, metaphorically speaking, due to years of austerity and other government policies. The Devons were about to find an empty coffer in reality. And yet her stomach was still churning as Dennis answered.

'She'll be nine this summer. She's a bit of a one-off. Heavily into ghosts and ghouls and vampires and zombies. Christmas at Wynter House was heaven on earth as far as she was concerned. The place has secret passages and what was once a priest hole.'

'I can't wait to see the place.' Cat glanced at Mary. 'Rafe did say we'd be welcome anytime. But I'm not sure how Olivia Wynter might react.'

Dennis nodded. 'I don't think anyone is sure how Olivia will react to any situation. Rafe and Adam and everyone else made us all feel welcome when we stayed there, but Olivia definitely did not. But I'm forgetting she's your grandmother. I apologise.'

'No need.' Cat threw him a smile.

'Right,' Amias said. 'Let's get started, shall we?'

Cat, Mary and Kyra left them to it. Kyra served the croissants she'd taken from the oven and despite Cat's anxiety, she ate two, with butter and raspberry jam slathered on top, while Amias and Dennis worked, turned the air blue with colourful language more than once, and finally yelled that they were ready to go into the cellar.

Cat was the first to the larder.

'You be careful, Amias. And you too, Dennis.'

Amias grinned. 'We'll need a ladder. Do you have one, Mary? If not, Dennis said he'll pop next door and get his.'

'There's a step ladder somewhere, I believe.'

'I'll go and get one of mine,' Dennis said. 'It'll only take a tick.'

He was next door and back before Amias had time to drink a cup of coffee, but Dennis stopped for one too, so it was about twenty minutes before they climbed down into the cellar, followed closely by Kyra and Cat. Cat hadn't intended to go down there but curiosity got the better of her.

'I'm curious too, Catherine.' Mary pulled a face. 'But I am definitely not going down that ladder. Especially as my ankle has only just healed properly.'

Amias shone the powerful torch that Mary had given him while he was having coffee. She had pulled it from one of the kitchen drawers. Dennis had also brought an equally powerful torch and together, the cellar was as bright as if there had been an electric light in there.

'It's not as damp down here as I'd expected,' Amias said.

'The fact that it's been closed up, plus the heating above has no doubt helped to keep it dry.' Dennis rocked one of the chairs back and forth. 'It seems pretty sound.'

Amias stood in front of the coffer. 'It's got a lock.'

Kyra coughed and waved a large iron key in her fingers. 'Perhaps this will help.' She handed it to Amias.

'Where did you find that?' Cat asked.

'It was hanging on a hook on the wall behind the ladder we came down. I spotted it right away.'

'Shall I do the honours?' Amias put the key in the lock and waited.

'Get on with it,' Mary yelled from above.

Cat took Kyra's hand and squeezed it tight.

A scraping sound was followed by a heavy click and Amias gingerly lifted the lid.

'I'll try to do this carefully in case the hinges break. It may not have been opened for centuries.'

He finally rested the top of the lid against the wall behind the coffer and they all looked inside.

'There's something wrapped in cloth,' said Cat, stating the obvious.

'It's muslin, I believe,' Dennis said.

'I think it's a painting or a picture of some sort judging by the shape,' Kyra offered.

'Shall we unwrap it here, or take it up for Mary?' Amias glanced at Cat.

'See if there's anything else in there and then we'll take it up to Mum. I think it's only fair that she sees whatever it is first.'

Amias lifted the wrapped item and held it away from his clothes.

'Nothing else,' Kyra said, peering around him. She sounded disappointed.

'This isn't heavy. Do you and Kyra want to take it up while Dennis and I move the coffer? I assume you want that brought up and not left here for several more centuries. These things are often worth a fair amount, depending on the age and quality and this looks in good condition. Natalia's always wanted a coffer, so if you and Mary want to sell it, I'm sure she and Josh will make you a very good offer and of course we'd have it valued first. But we can discuss that later.'

'I don't want it and I don't think Mum will. Kyra?'

Kyra shook her head. 'Nope. Your sister's welcome to it as far as I'm concerned.'

Cat grimaced at the discoloured cloth around the item but Kyra tutted and took it from Amias. It was about one metre by a half a metre and definitely looked like it was a picture of some sort. Kyra turned to go upstairs and Cat followed her, holding the ladder steady as Kyra climbed the steps, the object held against her.

'We think it's a picture or painting, Gran. Shall I put it on the table?'

'Good heavens, no! That cloth has probably been down there for years. It might be riddled with bacteria. Put it on the kitchen floor. At least we can wash off anything that lands on the tiles.'

'We should wait for Amias and Dennis,' Cat said. 'They're moving the coffer.'

'Tell them to do that later. I want to see what this is.'

Cat called to them and they hurried up to the kitchen.

Mary put on a pair of rubber gloves and carefully picked at a knot in the muslin. It wouldn't undo until Kyra handed her a pair of scissors. Mary unravelled reams of cloth, lifting and turning the object as necessary until the final piece of muslin was removed, revealing the back of a picture frame and canvas. A very old picture frame, gilded with what was clearly gold leaf around the edges and no doubt, the front.

'What does that say on the back of the canvas?' Kyra asked.

Mary peered at it and so did Cat. Cat was the first to decipher the scrawl.

'It says *Moonbeams Kiss*.'

Amias made a choking sound and dashed closer.

'It says what?' He sounded as if he were in pain and being strangled. 'Turn it over, Mary. I need to see the other side.'

Mary gave him a startled look but she did as he demanded and Cat watched the colour drain from his face as he stared at the painting. A beautiful, if a little faded, oil painting of a couple kissing on a sandy beach that looked a lot like Merriment Bay. They were wrapped in each other's arms and wearing what Cat knew to be Georgian attire, from the many Sunday evening historical dramas she'd watched on TV. Two beams of moonlight spread across a silver sea and met behind the couple on the sand, as if the moonbeams too were kissing.

'Amias?' Cat asked, anxiously studying his expression. 'What is it? What's wrong? Do you know something about this painting?'

All eyes turned to him but he didn't answer until Cat reached out and touched his arm. He tensed at her touch and he didn't take his gaze from the painting. He shook his head and his voice was little more than a whisper when he finally spoke.

'It can't be. It can't. What is it doing here?'

'Amias?' Cat tried again. 'What do you mean by "It can't be"? It can't be what?'

Now he looked at her and there was sorrow

and doubt and disbelief all mixed into one in his eyes.

'*Moonbeams Kiss*. The painting. It can't be the real one. The original. The one that disappeared in the summer of 1826. The one my ancestor, Titus Wells was accused of stealing. The one that made him the prime suspect in the disappearance of Jerusalem Raine, the young woman who owned the painting, and was the daughter of Obadiah Raine, the then vicar of Merriment Bay. The one that led to Titus being tried for Jerusalem's murder, even though her body was never found. He was hanged in February 1827, right here in Merriment Bay and all because of that painting. It can't be genuine. It must be a copy. But that just doesn't make sense. It must be a mistake. Because if it isn't, and bearing in mind it was hidden away in a boarded-up cellar beneath the floor of this house, it can only mean one thing.' He shot a look at Cat and Mary and Kyra before his gaze returned to the painting. 'It can only mean that someone in the Devon family had the painting all along and didn't want it to be found.'

Chapter Eight

It took a long walk on the beach, and a phone call to his sister before Amias could calm down enough to discuss the painting with his dad. He couldn't discuss it any further with Cat until he'd spoken to Alwick. Alwick knew the family history far better than Amias or Natalia ever had.

'What did Cat say when you told her the story?' Natalia handed Amias the large glass of wine that her husband Josh had poured him and took a gulp from her own glass as she snuggled down in a plush armchair in her sitting room.

Amias shook his head. 'What could she say? She didn't know anything about it and nor did Mary. They were almost as astonished as I was. And of course they were sure that no relative of theirs could've committed such a heinous crime as stealing the painting and letting someone else take the blame. And they may be right. Perhaps one of the Devons got hold of the painting afterwards. Dennis agreed that was a possibility.'

'Dennis?' Josh queried.

'Dennis Grey. Mary's neighbour. He was the one who discovered the cellar.'

Natalia nodded. 'We sold him and his wife their new house. Lovely couple. Their daughter is–'

'The new owner of The Mane Event,' Amias interrupted. 'I know. You've told me that more than once and I met her briefly on Boxing Day and properly yesterday.'

'But why was it hidden in the cellar, which was also hidden, if that was the case?' Josh asked. 'Surely they would've simply said they got it after Titus was hanged, and explained where they had got it from? Cat's ancestors, I mean.'

Amias nodded. 'That's exactly what Dennis said. The boards are Elizabethan, and no doubt from the earlier house that stood where Devon Villa stands now. But the footprint of both houses might not be the same. The boards could've been moved from elsewhere in the old house and used to board up the cellar at any time. We have no idea and no way of finding out. It could've been sealed up many years after the painting disappeared in 1826. But why would anyone need to hide the painting years later? That's the question. And the answer is, they wouldn't.'

Natalia frowned. 'Perhaps they wanted to keep it, and they thought they might have to give it back to the Raine family. You have to return stolen goods, don't you, even if you buy them in good faith?'

Josh shrugged. 'I don't know. But it does sound very fishy. Is the current incumbent of St. Mary-in-the-Fields, a direct descendant of this Jerusalem woman, or I suppose, her dad, Obadiah?'

'I was going to ask that,' Natalia said. 'And also, why did they all have such peculiar names? Titus is bad enough.'

Amias sighed. 'Let's not go off on a tangent, Nat. Dad's name isn't exactly run of the mill, is it? And neither is mine. Who cares what they were called or why? What's important is why that bloody painting was hidden in Devon Villa and who put it there?'

The door chime rang out.

'That sounds like Dad,' Natalia said, staying curled up in her armchair. 'He always rings the bell like that.'

'I'll let him in, shall I?' Josh shook his head, got up from the sofa and pressed the entry buzzer.

Alwick strode into the room, after dashing up the stairs, tapped Josh on the arm, planted a kiss on Natalia's head and ruffled Amias' hair as if Amias were a young child again. He then dropped into another armchair and smiled when Josh handed him a bottle of beer.

'So what's this about then? Why the family meeting? Please don't tell me Cat Devon has run off again. Although nothing would surprise me with the Devons.'

Amias sighed. 'Don't start, Dad. Cat hasn't gone anywhere. I know you still don't believe this but she really does love me.'

Alwick grinned. 'I do believe it, son. I was teasing. I saw how the pair of you behaved on New Year's Eve and I've seen you together several times since. She's as crazy about you as you are about her. I don't doubt that for a minute.'

'Oh.' Amias was surprised by that. 'That makes things a bit easier. But I don't want you to get on your high horse about how you can never trust a Devon, especially not a Devon woman, OK? I've got something to tell you, but it has nothing to do with Cat, Kyra or Mary. Or even Viola. This happened long before their time.'

Alwick furrowed his brows. 'I'm listening.'

Amias regaled him with details of how they'd found the cellar and the painting, and he handed Alwick his phone. 'I took photos of it. Front and back. It definitely looks like it's old, so it must be the original, but I'm no art expert.'

Alwick studied the photos in silence. He flopped back in the chair, took a swig of beer and sighed.

'Those bloody Devons. Oh don't worry. I'm not blaming the living. Just the family in general. This probably means that one of that bunch stole the painting and let Titus swing for Jerusalem's murder. Perhaps it was a Devon who killed her? Have you thought of that?'

Amias sighed once more. 'I've thought of everything, Dad, believe me. I've thought of nothing else since I saw the thing this morning. Being descended from the last man in Merriment Bay to be executed at a public hanging, and for a crime he maintained he didn't commit, and having that story told to me over the years, stayed with me. I felt as if I was the one standing on the gallows when I saw it. But there might be other possibilities.'

'There might. But I doubt it. I'd be willing to stake my house on the Devons being up to their necks in this. What are you going to do?'

'Do? What do you mean? What can I do? They're all long dead, Dad. I can't exactly ask them. Cat says she's pretty sure the canvas is old. The back is a dark beige with patches of mottled brown which, although that can be faked, looks genuine. And the weave is more open than more modern weaves, but as she says, she's an artist, not an art expert, either. We'd have to get a professional to look at it to be absolutely certain. I just wanted you and Natalia to hear this from me. You know what this place is like. Once the rumour mill starts there'll be all sorts of gossip. The story about you and Mary will no doubt rear its ugly head again. Although I've got good news on that front. Rafe and Adam met Cat and Kyra yesterday, and they're happy about everything. They're going to be making their relationship public knowledge.'

'They're going to accept her and Kyra as family?' Alwick looked surprised. 'Did Olivia agree?'

Amias shrugged. 'I don't think so. But it's not really her call now, is it? Rafe's head of the Wynter family now. He's the one who makes all the decisions regarding the family name and the Estate. Although he'd always run his decisions by Adam first. He's not as autocratic as Olivia. He takes his brother's feelings, and where possible, other people's, into account. But he and Adam both want to welcome Cat and Kyra to the Wynter family, so Olivia will have to go along with the majority decision whether she likes it or not.'

'Good for them.' Alwick raised his beer bottle in the air. 'I thought they'd do the right thing if they ever found out, but I wasn't sure that day would ever come until Cat came home to Merriment Bay. I'm glad it's all out in the open. I bet Mary's a bit peeved though. How's she coping after losing Viola and being scammed by that Jeremy guy? I've only seen her once, very briefly since then.'

'She's changed. Sometimes she gets quite emotional. But most of the time she tries to keep it all bottled up and is her usual, snobby self. Although now that I'm with Cat, Mary's attitude just makes me smile. I didn't find it amusing in the past, but now it is. Cat's been worried about her. Mary was with us when Cat met Rafe and Adam yesterday, and they were friendly to her. I think that helped, but she's been going through quite a tough time what with losing Viola and then Jeremy taking her for a ride. Rafe and Adam didn't hold a grudge towards me either, so that was good. But now we have this to contend with. You don't seem that concerned about it, Dad. I thought you'd be incandescent with rage.'

'I'm cross. Of course I am. But I'm mellowing in my old age. I would like to get to the bottom of this though. Oh. It seems I have got to the bottom of my beer.' He peered into the bottle and grinned.

'I'll get you another,' Josh said, getting up. 'And yes, darling. I'll top up the wine glasses.'

Natalia winked at Josh before glancing at Alwick. 'You're taking this far better than either of us expected, Dad. We thought you'd be off to Devon Villa with a shotgun.'

'A month ago, I might have. Now that Amias and Cat are together, the Devons are family, whether I like that or not. As he said, there's nothing any of us can do to bring the culprit to justice, or to bring Titus back. But we may possibly be able to find a way to clear Titus' name. That would mean something. All of our family has been tarred with the brush from Titus' public hanging. We've been seen as peasants, paupers, or simply poor by most of the residents of Merriment Bay throughout the generations. Being labelled as thieves, and by some, murderers, in addition, because Titus was hanged for both in 1827 has been an added cross to bear. You, Amias and I have managed to achieve a great deal of respect, not that it really matters what others think of us. It's what we think of ourselves that's important. But even so, the noose wasn't just put around poor Titus' neck. It's been hanging around our family name ever since. We may or may not be able to do something about that, but there is something we can do to authenticate the painting. And we don't need to take it to some fancy art expert in London or somewhere.'

'Oh? What?' Amias glanced at Natalia.

'We can take it to the rectory. Not to Bartholomew. To his nephew Francis, who often comes to visit and who I happen to know is coming down this weekend. I saw Constance the other day and she told me. Francis is helping Bartholomew write the Raine family history, so he'll know all about Jerusalem's disappearance. He also happens to be a freelance art conservator who is so well respected, according to Constance, he can write his own cheque, but as this painting once belonged to his family, he'll probably do it for free. Are the Devons going to give it back to the Raines? Or are they hoping to find a way to keep it?'

'I have no idea. I was so surprised, confused and frankly all over the place emotionally, that I didn't think to ask. I just told Cat I needed to take some time to clear my head and I'd see her later.'

'You'd better ask her before we mention anything to the Raines then,' Natalia said. 'Or things may get a little frosty between you and Cat if you go behind her back.'

'I would never do that. I'll speak to her the moment I leave here.'

'Then there's nothing we can do until you've done so.' Alwick glugged down his beer. 'I must go. I've got a lunch date. Keep me informed, son. If there's anything I can do to help, just give me a shout. Thanks for the beers, Josh.' He got to his feet, smiling broadly.

'Hold on just a minute, Dad,' Natalia said, reaching out to grab his hand as he walked past her chair. 'This is very unlike you. All smiles and patience in the face of such a discovery. When you say "lunch date", what exactly do you mean?'

His smile broadened. 'That's for me to

know and for you to wonder about.'

'Dad?' Natalia persisted.

He burst out laughing. 'Oh all right. I've got a date.'

'With a woman?' Josh sounded stunned.

Alwick laughed louder. 'Yes. With a woman.'

Amias couldn't believe his ears. 'That's fantastic news. Anyone we know?'

'Yes. It's Annie.'

'Annie? The waitress from Bella Vista?' Josh asked.

'I like her.' Natalia raised her glass. 'Well done, Dad. It's about time you got back out there.'

Amias grinned. 'Isn't she a friend of Mary's? That'll go down like a lead balloon. But I'm really pleased for you, Dad.'

'I believe Mary knows. I understand that Annie told her the other day. We've been seeing one another since the start of this year, but we didn't want to make it public knowledge until we were sure it was more than just a one-night stand.'

Natalia gasped. 'You slept with her before you starting dating? But more importantly, when were you going to tell us? It's pretty grim that Mary Devon knew before we did.'

Alwick shrugged. 'I've told you now. The only reason Annie wanted Mary to know was because of our … history. She knows Mary and

I aren't exactly friends. Although as I said, Mary's sort of family now. And those are words I never expected to hear myself say. As for having sex before we were technically dating, we're both adults. We were both single. It was one of those things. I'd popped in for a pizza and stayed longer than expected. I offered to walk her home when the restaurant closed and we ended up at my place instead. We were friends years ago. And Annie was also a friend of your mother's, don't forget. We all used to hang out together long before I married Gina. When Annie's last marriage fell apart and she decided to return here, I helped her get the job at Bella Vista. Not that that's relevant to this. But it's not as if we were total strangers. That's what I'm saying.'

'You're far from strangers now,' Josh said, grinning. 'Good for you. We'll have to invite you round for dinner. And you and Cat, Amias.'

'Oh joy,' Amias said. 'I'm joking. That's a great idea. It's odd that Cat didn't mention it to me though.'

Alwick shook his head. 'Perhaps Mary hasn't told her yet. That woman's good at keeping secrets. All the Devon women are.'

Chapter Nine

Alwick was right. Cat didn't know Annie was dating Amias' dad.

'Why didn't you tell me, Mum?' she asked Mary, when Amias broke the news on his return to Devon Villa.

Mary tutted and refilled her tea cup from the pot on the kitchen table.

'Because I didn't think it was important and I've had other things on my mind. I half expected it to be over in a few weeks anyway, so there wasn't much point.'

'Why should it be over in a matter of weeks?'

'Because I know Annie. And I know Alwick. People often think they've found love, only to find that all they've got is a snake.'

Amias frowned. 'Are you saying my dad's a snake, Mary? Because I'd have to take issue with that, I'm afraid.'

'Of course not. Don't be an imbecile. You

know fine well who I was referring to.' She poured him some tea and slid the cup and saucer towards him. 'What did Alwick say about the painting? I assume you've told him and Natalia. I'm surprised he didn't come charging in here with you and start accusing we Devons of all sorts of heinous crimes.'

'I have. And so am I, to be honest. But he took it rather well. He'd like to solve the mystery of how the painting found its way to a hidden cellar beneath Devon Villa. As we all would. And he hopes that we might find something to help clear Titus' name. He did have a suggestion. He also had a question.'

'Well spit it out, man.'

'Mum. Be nice.' Cat threw Mary a warning look.

'I am being nice. I'd vowed I'd never let Amias Wells set foot in this house and yet here he is at my kitchen table, dating my only daughter and drinking tea and chatting. Since Christmas he's been in and out of this place more times than I can recall, and last night he spent the night here. If that's not me being nice then I don't know what is.'

Amias laughed. 'You've made me feel as if Devon Villa is a second home, Mary. Anyway. Dad said that Bartholomew Raine's nephew is an art conservator and suggested you could ask him to authenticate the painting. His name's Francis and he often comes to stay with

Constance and Bartholomew. I think I may have met him. He's helping the vicar write the Raine family history, so he'll also have information about Jerusalem Raine, and possibly several others. But if you do ask him, the Raines might, theoretically, ask for the return of the painting. It did belong to Jerusalem, after all and it was believed to have been stolen.'

'Not necessarily,' Kyra said. 'I've been thinking about this all morning. What if the painting wasn't stolen? What if Jerusalem gave it to one of the Devons who was living here at the time? She disappeared, so no one could ask her. What if she sold the painting to them and ran away with the proceeds? Perhaps she'd sworn them to secrecy? Perhaps her father was cruel and strict. Obadiah is a mean-sounding name. Perhaps she was terrified he'd go after her?'

'Wow. You really have given this some thought.' Cat smiled.

'All of that is possible, in theory.' Amias put his cup to his mouth but hesitated to drink. 'But you're forgetting one thing. The Devons would've come forward after Titus was arrested. At least they would have if they were innocent in all of this. They wouldn't have let a man hang for a murder they knew hadn't happened. Would they?'

Mary sighed. 'Without knowing the family

history and who was in this house at the time, it's impossible to say.'

'Perhaps the animosity between the Devons and the Wells family goes back farther than you thought,' Kyra added. 'Perhaps they were happy to see Titus hanged. Although that is pretty awful, so I don't think we should dwell on that.'

'Do we have any family records?' Cat asked. 'Has anyone researched the family tree or anything? There must be records of who lived here back then. Aren't those things online these days?'

'Another mystery to solve.' Kyra sounded excited. 'Let's hope no one dies this time. Sorry. I didn't mean to say that. That sounded awful.'

Mary patted Kyra's hand. 'Awful, but true, sweetheart. Although all parties involved in this mystery are dead already, so that's some comfort.'

Amias smirked. 'Not for Titus it isn't.'

'But if we can prove his innocence,' Cat said. 'That will at least set the record straight.'

'Assuming he was telling the truth,' Mary added. 'Don't scowl at me, Catherine. People do lie, you know. We've all seen that more than once in recent months. Viola and Bailey lied. Jeremy lied. Even your beloved Kyle lied.'

Cat tensed at the mention of Kyle's name. It was true; he had lied. But he was Kyra's dad and his lie had been made with the best intentions. Cat wasn't going to let Mary drag his name through the mud.

'Yes. And let's not forget to add you to that list, Mum.'

'OK,' Amias said, giving Cat a quick kiss on her cheek. 'We agreed to put all that behind us. Let's get back to the painting and the question. Are you going to give the painting back to the Raines or are you planning to keep it, at least until we have more facts?'

Cat glanced at Kyra and Mary. 'I don't want to keep it. It's a beautiful painting but the more I've looked at it this morning, the more I think there's something very sad about it. It's not up to me though.'

'I think it's sad too,' Kyra agreed. 'But it's also very beautiful and it may be worth a lot of money. On the other hand, the fact that it was hidden means it wasn't loved as it should've been. It should be hanging on a wall somewhere. I think it should go back to the Raines, if I get a vote in what happens to it.'

'Then we're all agreed.' Mary scraped the feet of her chair across the floor as she stood up. 'I don't want the painting. It's been making me feel uneasy all morning. I'm loathe to say this because you'll all think I'm going mad, but I swear the thing has been sending me messages and I'd like that to stop. The sooner it leaves this house, the happier I will be.'

'Messages?' Kyra asked. 'What sort of

messages?'

'The sort I'd rather not hear. The sort that tell me this painting isn't the only discovery we'll make. That there's more to this than we know.'

'There was nothing else in the coffer, Gran.'

'I know. But I've still got a nasty feeling that we've stumbled on something unpleasant. Literally in my case, bearing in mind that it was me tripping on that loose board that started all this. I have an uneasy feeling that that was meant to happen. And let's not forget, I've been having strange dreams ever since that night I tripped on that damn board.'

'But why now?' Cat asked. 'If what we're assuming is correct and that painting has been hidden for at least a couple of centuries, why would these *messages* only be sent now? And why to you?'

'If I knew the answer to that, Catherine, we wouldn't be having this conversation, would we? I think we should give Bartholomew a call and ask him and Constance to come round for dinner tonight. They may be able to shed some light on the matter. And unless you have any objection, Amias, I think we should tell them to take the thing with them.'

'Why would I object?' Amias looked surprised. 'I have no say in the matter.'

'It was your ancestor who hanged for it.

That gives you some say, as far as I'm concerned.'

'Strictly speaking, Titus was hanged for Jerusalem's murder, not the theft of the painting. He would've faced deportation to Australia for that. But thank you, Mary. I appreciate it. I agree with everyone else. The Raines should have the painting. After all, it did belong to them.'

Chapter Ten

'We couldn't possibly take it, could we my love?'

Bartholomew Raine looked at his wife and shook his head of thinning grey hair as he sipped his sherry.

'Absolutely not.' Constance straightened her back against the chair and placed her now empty tea cup and saucer on the table in the kitchen of Devon Villa. 'It isn't ours to take. Of course, we can't speak for Francis. He may feel differently. If we'd known what this was about, we would've asked if he could join us.'

'We could call him, I suppose,' Bartholomew suggested.

'That's a good idea. Shall we do that? May we ask him to join us?'

Constance looked around the table and Cat glanced at Amias, Kyra and Mary.

Mary coughed lightly. 'We'd rather hoped to be rid ... I mean, we'd hoped you'd take it with you this evening. Your nephew lives in London, I believe.'

'He does.' Bartholomew smiled. 'But he could be here in a trice, couldn't he my love?'

Constance nodded. 'He could.'

'From London?' Kyra asked, giving the vicar and his wife the oddest look.

'From the rectory.'

'The rectory?' Mary repeated.

'Is he already in Merriment Bay?' Amias said. 'I thought he was coming down at the weekend. Dad mentioned he'd spoken with you.'

'The dear boy arrived last night.' Bartholomew grinned at his wife. 'Francis often begins his weekend on a Thursday evening. One of the joys of being self-employed, he tells us.'

'Oh dear God, then yes,' Mary said. 'Please call him and ask him to join us. I wished you'd said he was here. I would've invited him, regardless. He must think I'm very rude to exclude him.'

Bartholomew frowned. Probably due to Mary's little blasphemy.

'Not at all, Mary. He didn't mind one bit. He's perfectly happy with his own company. More's the pity. We wish he'd find himself a nice young lady to settle down with. He's twenty-eight you know. But he's happy with his life and tells us there's plenty of time for all that. He did bring a lovely young lady here at Christmas. I can't recall her name. I have a dreadful memory for names, don't I my love?'

Constance nodded. 'You do, dear. Her name was Sarah. Sweet little thing, but very clingy. Not at all the type of girl that Francis needs. But I don't think anyone wants to hear about our dear nephew's love life. I believe they want you to give Francis a call and request his presence with some urgency.'

'Ah yes. This may come as a bit of a shock to him. Jerusalem is one of his pet projects. Well, the mystery of her disappearance, at least. He descends from her line, you know. That's why we feel he should be the one to decide about the painting, not us.' Bartholomew put his phone to his ear and waited for an answer.

'Wait.' Kyra sat upright. 'Are you saying Jerusalem had a child? Was she married? I thought she was the daughter of Obadiah Raine. Was the child illegitimate?'

'Goodness no!' Constance looked stunned. 'Jerusalem was Obadiah's child. That's correct. But she was married to one of her cousins. A distant cousin, but a Raine, nonetheless. So she was a Raine before and after her wedding. Her son was born within the year, and that's the line from which Francis descends.'

'He's not a direct nephew of yours then?' Amias asked.

'Oh, he is.' Constance beamed and her cheeks puffed out with pride. 'That's what makes him so special to both of us. He descends from the Raines, on his father's side, although distant from Bartholomew's family. But his father, by chance, met and married my younger sister. So Francis is also my nephew by blood.'

'Eew,' Kyra said. 'Sorry. But that sounds a little odd.'

Constance smiled. 'It does sound rather scandalous, doesn't it? But it's not. Far from it. Just a quirk of Fate. Until he met my dear sister, God rest her soul, Francis' father, whose name was Trevor, had never met Bartholomew, or even knew of his existence. That's how distant the relationship was.'

'They say that if we trace our lineage back far enough, we're all related,' Cat said.

'You said 'was Trevor' and also 'God rest her soul' so does that mean that your nephew's parents are both dead?' Kyra asked.

Constance nodded. 'For several years, now.'

'Ah. Francis dear boy,' Bartholomew boomed out. 'Drop everything and join us for dinner at Devon Villa, will you? We're in the depths of a mystery that you'll find enthralling. It involves Jerusalem and the *Moonbeams Kiss*. Yes. Yes. That's right. I said Jerusalem and the missing painting. In fact, I'm looking at the painting as we speak. Hello? Francis? Oh. I do believe he's rung off. He's no doubt on his way right now. He should be here very soon.'

'Does he know where Devon Villa is?' Kyra asked.

'Oh dear.' Bartholomew rubbed his chin. 'I don't know if he does. I know I mentioned how lovely it was and that it overlooks the sea.'

'He'll call back if he doesn't,' Amias said, a mere second before the vicar's phone rang again.

'Hello. Yes dear boy. It's in Channel View Lane. The second house along. We'll see you very soon.'

'I'll go and wait for him at the door.' Kyra laughed as she got up. 'He might race right past in his excitement. You said he's twenty-eight. Any distinguishing features?'

'He's very handsome,' Constance said, smiling proudly. 'His hair is a warm brown and his eyes are as blue as a tropical ocean. Not that you'll see those from a distance.' She gave a little laugh. 'He'll be wearing a Royal blue coat and a turquoise scarf. I bought him the scarf for Christmas. But don't stand out in the cold, dear. I'm sure he'll find us. He's very bright.'

'I want to get some fresh air, anyway. It's so warm in here tonight, what with the oven on, fires in both the sitting and dining rooms, and the radiators on full pelt. I'm beginning to melt.'

'It's the end of January,' Mary said. 'The heating needs to be on.'

'Put a coat on or you'll catch a chill,' Cat said.

Chapter Eleven

Kyra ignored Cat's advice. The temperature inside Devon Villa was stifling and she was glad to be outside even if there was a distinct chill in the air. She stood on the doorstep and glanced across the road to the sea but there was no moon, and as it was already dark, she could only see a black expanse of water and hear the swooshing of the waves against the shore.

She looked to her left, but there were no pedestrians on Channel View Lane as yet. Perhaps Francis wasn't as keen to get to Devon Villa as Constance and Bartholomew had thought he would be. The walk from the rectory would only take a few minutes, door to door, for someone young and fit. But perhaps Francis wasn't fit. Both Constance and Bartholomew were overweight. Especially Bartholomew. Francis might be more so. Or perhaps he'd got lost. For someone who was supposed to be bright, it was a bit foolish to hang up the phone without knowing where you were going.

She skipped down the steps and walked slowly towards Coast Road. Headlights beamed from cars driving past in each direction, but still there was no sign of Francis Raine. Maybe he was a slow walker. She continued on until she reached the junction, looking from left to right and back down Channel View Lane, although there was no way she could have missed him.

Should she turn right and walk towards the rectory, in the hope of meeting him on the way, or turn back towards the house and wait for him to get there? It was colder than she'd expected and a sudden shiver shot through her.

She'd just decided to go home when she saw a man running along Coast Road from the left. The street lamps spotlighted his Royal blue coat, and as he ran, a turquoise scarf flapped around his neck and shoulders. He definitely didn't take after Constance or Bartholomew. Neither of them could run that fast; assuming they could run at all. He carried a laptop case in one hand, and a plastic carrier bag with *Merry Shopper* emblazoned across it, in the other. If this was Francis Raine, he had clearly made a detour to the supermarket.

Kyra waited for him beneath the street lamp on the corner of Channel View Lane, smiling and raising a hand in greeting as he approached.

'Hello. I've been waiting for you. My name's Kyra.'

He slowed his pace but didn't stop.

'Oh. Er. Thanks. But no thanks. Sorry. Have a good night.'

She watched open mouthed as he ran past, veering around her and dashing onto Channel View Lane.

'Hey! Hold on.'

He threw her a crooked smile over his shoulder and continued on his way. 'Sorry. People are waiting for me.'

'And I'm one of them!'

He stopped suddenly and turned, sighing visibly.

'Look. You're a stunning girl, and I don't mean to be rude. But I do have people waiting. I can give you money for a cup of coffee and something to eat, but that's all.'

Kyra blinked rapidly several times.

'What? I'm not a beggar.'

He looked her up and down. 'I didn't think you were.'

Realisation dawned. 'Jesus Christ. You think I'm a hooker!'

'Er. Not necessarily. I do think, if you're going to hang around on street corners beneath lampposts, dressed as you are, most people will get that impression. But if you say you're not, I'll believe you. Here.' He pulled something from his pocket as he hurried back towards her and he handed her a ten-pound note. 'Go and get yourself something warm to eat and drink. And come to St. Mary-in-the-Fields tomorrow around 2 in the afternoon. We'll find you a coat. Then at least you can keep warm.'

His smile might be slightly crooked but it lit up his eyes, and Constance was right. They were the colour of a tropical ocean. Deep enough to drown in.

'Thanks.' Kyra smiled back, took the money and stuffed it in the pocket of her black velvet shorts, which she was wearing over a pair of thick black tights, along with the black suede, designer trainers Cat had bought her for Christmas. Well, the replacement pair. Jeremy ran off with the originals. 'You're very kind.'

'Think nothing of it. Listen. I know you probably don't want advice, but this is dangerous. You never know who might pick you up. I'm not going to lecture you, but I really hope you'll find a better way to spend your time. Sorry, but I really must go. Take care. And don't forget about St. Mary-in-the-Fields, 2 p.m. tomorrow. OK?'

'Got it.'

He smiled. 'I might see you soon then.'

'Sooner than you think.'

The lamplight highlighted a couple of creases around his eyes and for a second his brows furrowed as if he was having doubts about something, but he turned, waved goodbye and ran off towards Devon Villa.

Kyra burst out laughing, but covered her mouth with one hand so that Francis wouldn't hear her. Then she flicked her long ginger curls away from her face, tugged at her purple, bolero-style cardigan to cover her black low-cut T-shirt, and made her way back to the house.

She reached the foot of the steps just as Francis spotted her. He looked concerned and was about to speak when Cat opened the front door.

'There you are,' Cat said. 'What took you so long? We were getting a little worried. Why did you ring the bell?'

'Er.' Francis looked from Cat to Kyra and back again.

'Sorry, Mum.' Kyra ran up the stairs, grinning. 'I thought I'd lost my key. Francis, this is my mum, Cat Devon. Mum, this is Francis Raine. Gran was right. I should've worn a coat.'

She winked at Francis as she hurried past and Cat stepped aside to let them in.

'It's lovely to meet you, Francis. Do come in. Kyra will show you the way.'

'Shit,' he mumbled. 'I mean, thank you. It's good to meet you too. Er. These are for you. Thank you for inviting me.'

He handed the plastic bag to Cat, and Kyra stretched her neck in order to see what it contained.

'Wine, flowers and chocolates,' Kyra said, nodding appreciatively. 'It's been an expensive night so far and you've only just arrived.'

Cat gave Kyra an odd look but merely smiled and closed the door behind Francis.

'Thank you, Francis. There was no need for you to bring anything, but it's very thoughtful and extremely generous.'

'It's my pleasure.'

'Kyra will take your coat. Excuse me for a moment and I'll take these into the kitchen.'

A devilish grin spread slowly across Francis' mouth, and his eyes danced with amusement.

'This is a surprise.'

'I'll bet it is. If you think I'm giving you back your tenner, you're sadly mistaken. I don't think I've ever been so insulted in my life.' She tried to keep a straight face, but a broad grin tugged at her mouth,

'Really?' He looked her up and down, pointedly and provocatively.

'There's nothing wrong with the way I'm dressed.'

'I didn't say there was.'

'Yes, you did. You said I look like a hooker.'

'I said you gave that impression. And I don't think I actually used the word hooker. You did.'

'You didn't need to. Your holier than thou attitude said so much more than words ever could.' She tossed her head like a model in a shampoo advert, and pouted at him.

'Nice,' he said, still grinning. 'You've got gorgeous hair.'

'Too late for flattery. And I'm still keeping your tenner.'

'It was worth every penny.'

'Yeah. That's what they all say.' She batted her eyelashes and licked her lips.

He burst out laughing.

'Kyra?' Cat called from the kitchen.

'Just coming, Mum. Francis seems to be struggling.' Kyra grinned at him. 'Need a hand?'

His grin broadened. 'How much will it cost me?'

She raised her brows. 'A lot more than a tenner. Now hurry up. I'm starving.'

'Yeah.' He shrugged off his coat and scarf. 'That's what they all say.' He grinned again as he handed them to her. 'I want those back.'

'Then you'd better be nice to me.' She hung his things on the coat rack and wandered down the hall. 'Follow me.'

'And you'll lead me to temptation?'

'I'll lead you to the kitchen. Temptation will have to wait. Besides, I've got a boyfriend.'

'Don't they call those pimps?' He laughed as she turned and grinned at him.

'I don't know. I'll ask him tomorrow.'

'He's not here?'

'Nope. But that doesn't mean you can flirt with me in his absence.'

'Flirt with you? Who says I'm flirting with you?'

'I do. Now that you know I'm not a hooker. Sorry to burst your bubble, but you're really not my type.'

'Because I'm at least eight years older and dress conservatively?'

'Ten, from what I hear. But no. Your age isn't an issue.' She stopped, turned to face him, and slowly looked him up and down, tilting her head slightly to one side and biting on her bottom lip. He was wearing pale blue, heavy cotton chinos, a plain white, open-necked shirt, and a dark blue, V-neck sweater, together with a mischievous smile that sent tingles from the top of her head to the tips of her fingers. 'Your dress-sense is OK. For someone your age. It's your sanctimonious attitude that's the problem.'

'You certainly know how to make a man feel … uncomfortable.' He gave a little cough to clear his throat. 'I don't think trying to persuade a beautiful, and very sexy, young woman not to throw her life away is exactly sanctimonious. But we'll agree to disagree.'

Kyra winked at him and sashayed into the kitchen in the full knowledge that Francis would be watching her as he followed close behind.

'Francis! There you are dear boy. How thoughtful of you to pop to the shop. We thought you'd got lost.'

'Not lost, Uncle Bart. Merely led astray.'

Cat gave him and Kyra another odd look before smiling and indicating he should take a seat at the table.

'Let me introduce you to everyone. You've met my daughter Kyra, obviously. This is my mum, Mary. And this is my boyfriend, Amias. We're in here for now, but we'll be eating in the dining room. It's because we don't want to move the painting elsewhere.'

He nodded hello and smiled at everyone, but as soon as Cat mentioned the painting, he grew serious.

'May I see it, please? And may I ask how it came to be in your possession?'

'Gran tripped over a floorboard,' Kyra said.

'Excuse me?' He furrowed his brows.

'That's how it came to be in our possession. Gran tripped over a loose floorboard in the larder and when Amias and our neighbour took up the board we found a hidden cellar.'

He glanced from her to his uncle and aunt. 'Seriously?'

They nodded.

'Yes. And the Devons have very kindly offered it to us, dear boy. But of course we can't take it. Legally speaking, we believe it would belong to you.'

'To me?' He looked thoughtful. 'I think that's debatable. It was hidden in the cellar, you say?'

'We didn't know it was there,' Kyra said. 'Neither the painting nor the cellar. Both came as a surprise.'

'What?'

Cat coughed. 'We'll explain all that later. Here's the painting.' She pointed to the other side of the room, where the painting sat on several sheets of paper kitchen-towel, covered by its original wrapping, on a small wooden table, and was propped up against a wall. 'Please feel free to examine it.'

'Thank you.'

His eyes looked even brighter than before, and Kyra let out a little sigh, which she turned into a cough as soon as Cat glanced in her direction.

Kyra watched him as he twisted, turned and tapped the painting with his fingers. At one point, his face was so close to the canvas that his perfectly shaped nose almost touched it. He studied it from every angle, crouching down, standing up, leaning to one side and then the other. Finally, after several minutes, he turned to face his audience, seemingly surprised that everyone was staring at him.

'It's genuine. Without a doubt. It's the original *Moonbeams Kiss*. The one that disappeared from the rectory in the summer of

1826, along with Jerusalem Raine. Although there's no firm evidence that they disappeared together, of course. But they did disappear on the very same day.'

Chapter Twelve

'It's very kind of you,' Francis said, helping himself to some stilton from the cheeseboard at the end of dinner. 'And believe me, I would love to own the painting. But as I said earlier, I think we need to see if we can find out how the painting came to be in your cellar before we make any decisions regarding ownership. As Kyra suggested, there's a chance your ancestors acquired it in a perfectly honourable and innocent way. Jerusalem could have sold it, I suppose. But I don't believe she would have, and I'm certain she wouldn't have run off with someone.'

Kyra tutted. 'Why not? It isn't just romantic fantasy, you know. People run off together in real life. Mum and Dad did. At least they tried to. But Dad got killed, so Mum ran off later, on her own.'

Francis looked both surprised and confused. 'I'm so sorry.'

'There's no need.' Cat smiled at him. 'It was a long time ago. But people do run away. When Kyra mentioned the idea to us earlier today, it crossed our minds that it was possible.'

He nodded. 'Yes. But I don't believe Jerusalem did. You see, I have her journals. And she makes no mention of intending to run away.'

'Her journals?' Kyra was surprised. 'The woman kept a diary?'

'Many gentlewomen kept journals in those days.'

'I suppose they had little else to do,' Mary said.

Cat laughed. 'Other than wander around gardens, visit those worse off than them, go to parties, balls and dinners, play the pianoforte or whatever, read, paint or draw, and swoon every so often. I'm joking. I expect many women led very busy lives.'

Francis shook his head. 'You've just described Jerusalem's life. Although balls were a rarity for her, but there were several country dances. She did attend one ball that I know of. She bemoans the fact that she isn't allowed to pursue a more worthwhile existence. But she was in an unusual position. At the age of nineteen, she was married off to a distant cousin she hardly knew. Edward Raine was a naval officer and after spending little more than a week together after their wedding, he went back to sea, and she remained at the rectory. Edward couldn't afford a home of their own and that had been part of the arrangement. Jerusalem's mother had died years earlier and Jerusalem effectively ran her father's house. She spent a great deal of her time visiting the poor, many of whom had been known to her all her life. She writes in detail about the appalling conditions in which so many of the families lived and also that she wanted to do all she could to improve things for them. But no one listened to women much in those days, especially a mere vicar's daughter.'

'Jane Austen was a vicar's daughter,' Kyra said. 'People listened to her.'

'People read her books, most of which are more about the wealthy than the impoverished. I'm not a fan. Elizabeth Gaskell, on the other hand, I enjoyed reading.'

'Criticising Austen is close to blasphemy.' Kyra scowled at him.

'I wasn't criticising. I simply said I'm not a fan. I didn't say she wasn't a talented writer. But getting back to Jerusalem. She soon discovered she was pregnant, and that seemed to change everything. Her journal entries became less frequent after her son was born, and more like the ramblings of someone in turmoil. She writes several times that she feels as if she is being driven out of her mind. It's really odd. And quite surprising. Sadly, there are very few entries in the months leading up to her disappearance, and what there are don't give any clues as to what may have happened to her.'

'Do you think she was losing her mind?' Cat asked. 'Because if she was, isn't there a small chance that she could've taken her own life?'

Francis shook his head. 'I suppose there is that possibility, but I honestly don't believe she would have done so. She adored her son and would never have left him. But we'll never know what happened.'

Amias frowned. 'Was this mentioned at Titus' trial? I haven't read the records, but I think Dad has. I don't recall him saying anything about such a possibility. But if her journals said she felt that way, why wasn't that considered?'

Francis bit his lip, and Kyra smiled. She sometimes bit her lip when she was thinking about something.

'Jerusalem's state of mind was never discussed. Her journals weren't used in evidence. Don't forget, there were no police as we know them today. The first 'proper' police force only came into being in 1829 in London. At the time of Jerusalem's suspected murder, there were merely private constables, a few paid night watchmen, and justices of the peace. And the Bow Street Runners, of course. Titus was tried at what was called an assize court, which was at least presided over by professional judges, unlike the courts of sessions, but courts of assizes were only held a couple of times a year in their own administrative counties. Trials were brief, witnesses were often paid to give evidence, and many officials, lawyers and witnesses were corrupt. A man like Titus, from a poor background, stood little chance of receiving a fair trial. He'd have effectively been found guilty long beforehand. And what I do know, from other letters and documents I've read, is that Obadiah Raine, George Devon, who lived in the house that was here at the time and was a justice of the peace, and would've been the one Jerusalem's disappearance and the theft of the painting were first reported to, and Richard Wynter, the assize judge at the murder trial, were all friends. In my opinion, Titus Wells never stood a chance.'

'Bloody hell,' Cat said.

Amias merely looked stunned, as did Mary. Kyra couldn't believe what she'd just heard.

'Are you saying that the three of them set Titus up? Three men who are related to several people sitting around this dinner table, set up Amias' ancestor? Isn't this all a bit of a weird coincidence? That the Devons, the Wynters, the Raines and the Wells are all connected to

Jerusalem's disappearance? Weren't there any other families living in Merriment Bay?'

Francis grinned. 'People didn't move around as much in those days. The Raines have lived here for centuries, as have the Devons and the Wells. The Wynters have lived in Wyntersleap for even longer. Merriment Bay wasn't much larger than Wyntersleap village in the 1700s. It had expanded a little by the early 1800s, but to answer your question, no. There probably weren't many more families living here in those days. The Lesters were here. And Squire James Johnson owned Merriment Bay Farm at the time, but his line died out and the Dove family moved in much later.'

'So everyone knew everyone else?' Cat said. 'Even more so than today. Surely someone must've known what happened to Jerusalem. She must've had friends. There must've been gossip. Or was the finger pointed at Titus from day one? And if so, what I don't understand is why.'

'Nor do I,' Amias said. 'Why was everyone so certain Titus had murdered her?'

Francis took a deep breath. 'Because he was in love with Jerusalem. And she was married to someone else.'

'What?' Amias looked incredulous. 'I didn't know that.'

'The court records state that he had been seen following her, and had accosted her on

110

more than one occasion. All that probably means is he'd stopped her in the street and talked to her. But that wasn't the done thing and people would've noticed. The truth is, there was probably far more between them than that. Titus admitted he was in love with her, although from memory that's not contained in the trial records. It's mentioned in other documents I've read. A letter from Obadiah to another relative. Obadiah had a habit of keeping a copy of every letter he sent. That meant writing them both out by hand. No copiers in those days. Carbon paper was invented in 1801, I believe, but Obadiah wouldn't have had any. Anyway, that was all Titus would say. He didn't really try to defend himself. Which is strange for an innocent man. And when he was found guilty and sentenced to death, he didn't rail against the judgement. He merely protested his innocence again, quietly and reasonably.

'You said there wasn't any point,' Cat said.

'But he didn't even try. He denied the theft of the painting and of murdering Jerusalem, but it was as if he didn't seem to care what became of him. And for an innocent man, that's weird. But for a man who was madly in love with a woman he knew was dead, that's not quite so odd.'

Amias glared at him. 'You're saying you think he did murder Jerusalem and he felt he deserved to pay for that? But if so, why would he say he was innocent?'

'I'm not saying he murdered her. I'm saying he was deeply in love with her. That he believed she was dead. And because of that, he didn't care if he lived or died. As he was led away, he was overheard to say that despite his innocence, he was content, as it meant he would see Jerusalem again. To those who heard those words, that proved beyond doubt that he knew she was dead and therefore must've been the one who killed her.'

'But you don't think he did?' Kyra asked. 'Do you think he knew who had killed her?'

Francis sighed. 'No. I think he just knew it wasn't him. I believe he and Jerusalem were lovers. Not necessarily in the physical sense. Although perhaps they were. I'm pretty sure they'd kissed. And I'll tell you why. The couple in the painting, *Moonbeams Kiss*, are Jerusalem and Titus. I know this because there are sketches of Titus in Jerusalem's journals. They're not of him on his own, of course. She couldn't have done that, for obvious reasons. They're sketches of labourers in the fields, or people walking along the shore, but in each one, the same dark-haired man appears. The same man that's in the painting. And the woman matches the description of Jerusalem almost exactly. I've seen reports of the hanging, and Titus is described in one or two. He's definitely the same man.'

'Oh my God!' Kyra shrieked. 'This just gets better. Or worse, depending on how you look at it.'

'I can't take this in,' Amias said, glancing at Cat and back to Francis. 'Are you sure?'

Bartholomew spoke for the first time in a while. 'Francis always checks his facts.'

Constance nodded. 'I've also read the journals and seen the sketches. Jerusalem definitely wasn't in love with her husband. Other than their wedding day, she rarely mentions him.'

'Hardly at all,' Francis confirmed. 'But she writes a great deal about the unfairness of social divides, and of arranged and loveless marriages. She also writes about her son. But the things she writes most about are how the sun shines on the fields of corn where labourers toil and sweat, of the great pleasure a walk along the shore gives her, as others frolic at the water's edge. Stuff like that. She never mentions Titus, but from her sketches, I think it's clear what – or who – she's really talking about in those otherwise innocent statements. She's watching him. And I'm pretty sure he's watching her right back.'

'Who painted *Moonbeams Kiss*?' Kyra asked.

'Didn't I say? Sorry. It was Jerusalem.'

'Really? Oh. It's not a valuable painting

then?'

Francis looked her directly in the eye.

'I think that depends on what one considers to be valuable. To me, the painting is priceless. I'm amazed it's in such good condition after being kept in that cellar for any number of years. The muslin would've helped protect it but even so. It's beyond anything I could've hoped for.'

'It was in a coffer.' Kyra met his look.

'A coffer? In the cellar?'

'We were going to bring it up,' Amias said. 'But I was so surprised when I saw the painting, that I completely forgot about the coffer and went for a walk to think. By the time I got back, Dennis, Mary's neighbour, had gone. It's heavy so it'll need two people to lift it.'

'I'm happy to help if you want to do it tonight.' Francis had an excited expression on his face. 'I'd like to see where the painting was kept. There may be other clues.'

'There aren't,' Kyra said. 'We looked.'

'You've just eaten, dear boy,' Bartholomew reminded Francis. 'You shouldn't be lifting things after a large meal. Which was delicious, by the way, ladies.' He smiled at Kyra, Cat and Mary.

'Kyra should take the credit,' Mary said. 'She did all the cooking.'

Francis grinned at Kyra. 'A woman of many talents.'

She laughed. 'You'd better believe it.'

'She's an artist too,' Mary said, beaming with obvious pride. 'Just like her mother. They're extremely talented. But they don't get that from me.'

'An artist?' Francis sounded surprised, but his expression was one of wonder and delight. 'We have something in common.'

'You're welcome to look at the coffer now if you like,' Cat said. 'You can examine it while your meal goes down.'

'That would be fantastic. Thank you.'

'I'll show you the cellar,' Amias said.

'I'll do it,' Kyra jumped up. 'You stay and have your coffee. I don't want any.'

Cat gave her another odd look, but she didn't say a word as Kyra led Francis from the dining room into the kitchen.

'I'm glad you offered,' he said when they were out of earshot of the others. 'I wanted to have a quiet word.'

'Oh. What about?'

'This boyfriend of yours. Is it serious?'

'Why?' She darted a look at him.

'Just curious.'

'You know what they say about curiosity.'

'But I'm not a cat. Are you studying art at uni? What do you like to paint?'

'So many questions. Here's the cellar.' She picked up the torch from one of the larder shelves where Amias had left it for later. She turned it on and shone the beam at the ladder. 'After you.'

He grinned. 'I would say ladies first, but it's probably best if I go ahead. Just in case.'

She tutted. 'Been there, seen it, nothing scary to report.'

'In that case, after you.'

'Stop being a prat and get down there, will you!'

'Beautiful, talented and oh so charming. Your boyfriend's a very lucky man.'

'He is.'

Francis grinned and hurried down the ladder.

'I'll catch you if you fall,' he beamed up at her.

'Get out of the way or I might just land on top of you.'

'That's the best offer I've had all night.'

'What? Better than the painting?'

'No. You're right. Second best offer.'

'Now who's charming?'

She clambered down and stopped in front of him as he stared into her eyes. For a moment she hesitated but then shoved him aside and marched towards the coffer, shining the torch at the front and the open lock.

'The key was hanging on the wall back there. It's weird. Why lock it and leave the key right there? And why leave it here in the first place? And why these two chairs?'

He grinned at her. 'So many questions.'

'Funny.'

'I'm an art conservator, not a detective, so I've no idea. But I do know this coffer is Jacobean. That dates it between 1603 and 1625. Much older than the painting. And it's a fine piece of furniture. Coffers can range in value, based on age, design and material. Most coffers are oak. Some are plain, some have intricate designs. This one's a beauty.'

'But it doesn't help us with the painting, does it?'

'No.'

Kyra wiped the seat of one of the chairs with the sleeve of her cardigan, ensuring the torch beam still shone on the coffer and Francis, who was now bending over the coffer, opening and closing the lid and feeling around the edges and sides with his fingers. She was about to sit down, but thought better of it. What if it gave way and she landed on her backside? Instead, she leant against the wall, wishing she had stopped at her third glass of wine and hadn't had the fourth. Or the glass of port with the cheese. Or did she have two glasses of port?

'Could you keep that torch steady, please? I'm trying to see if there's–'

A dull thud stopped him mid-sentence and he smiled up at her. She pushed herself away from the wall and moved closer.

'What was that? Have you broken something?'

'No. I've discovered something.'

He pushed at the wooden panel and a small, narrow drawer just a few inches square and about an inch deep, grudgingly inched its way out. Inside there appeared to be another piece of muslin, also folded into a square.

'What's that? A spare bit of muslin?'

He shook his head. 'It's paper.' He eased it out with his fingertips. 'And judging by the feel of it, paper from around the early 1800s.' He carefully unfolded it and studied the fading ink as Kyra moved closer and did the same.

'Can you read it? What does it say?' Kyra's heart was pounding in her chest but she tried to keep calm. 'I bet it's just a shopping list or something equally boring, isn't it? Francis? Francis, what's wrong? What did it say?'

He was staring at the seemingly solid sandstone ground in a bemused fashion, but when she reached out and took the mottled sheet of paper from his hand, he looked her in the eye.

'It's a confession. And it appears to indicate that Jerusalem is buried right beneath our feet.'

Kyra let out a horrified shriek as she instinctively jumped backwards. Her hand shot to her chest and she let the paper fall to the floor as she took a gasp of breath and composed herself.

'You have got to be kidding! If this is your idea of a joke, it's not bloody funny.'

Chapter Thirteen

Francis wasn't joking. And chaos immediately ensued in Devon Villa.

Kyra rushed back to the dining room, almost tumbling from the ladder in her haste, and breathlessly blurted out what Francis had found.

Francis followed close behind, the confession letter in his hand. It was passed around the table, Amias being the first to read the horrifying words. The only person who refused to read, or even touch it, was Mary. She turned deathly pale, gripped the edge of the table with both hands and declared that she couldn't spend the night in a house with a body buried beneath the floor.

'But we don't know if it's true,' Amias said. 'That floor looked fairly solid to me. And why would anyone write a murder confession, fold it up and hide it in a secret drawer in an old coffer? It must be some sort of tasteless practical joke, surely? Things like this just don't happen.'

'Why would anyone joke about such a thing?' Cat said, looking a little pale herself. 'And the painting was hidden in the coffer. We know it was stolen and we know Jerusalem disappeared.'

'That's the part that doesn't make much sense,' Francis said, a thoughtful expression on his face. 'Did he steal the painting and kidnap Jerusalem at the same time, then murder her in the cellar and hide the painting in the coffer? And then write a confession and hide that too. And if so, why? The painting had no real monetary value. It was definitely painted by Jerusalem. It's not exactly small, so to carry that and abduct Jerusalem at the same time would've taken some doing. Or more than one person. It just doesn't add up.'

'There's only one way to find out,' Kyra said, pouring glasses of brandy for herself and everyone else from the decanter on the table.

'Dig up the floor,' Amias said.

'Exactly.' Kyra dropped onto the chair she'd vacated less than twenty minutes earlier and emptied her glass in one long gulp.

'Shouldn't we call the police?' Constance asked, her hands shaking as she held her glass to her lips.

'For a possible murder committed almost two hundred years ago?' Amias looked doubtful.

'I'm not sure of the procedure for such an eventuality,' Bartholomew said. 'But I feel I should go down and say a few words, just in case, if you'll allow me.'

'Yes. Yes of course.' Cat nodded. 'Oh God. How awful. To think she's been there all this time.'

'Thank you, Catherine,' Mary said. 'But I'd really rather not think about it. I said something awful would come of this. I told you all this morning that I had a dreadful feeling about it. And then there were my dreams. I knew it wouldn't simply end with finding that painting.'

'Are you saying you think it was Jerusalem sending you those messages, Gran?' Kyra reached out and touched Mary's hand.

'Messages?' Bartholomew had got to his feet to go to the kitchen but he hesitated.

'Gran said she felt as if someone was sending her messages.' Kyra caught Francis' eye. 'You don't believe any of this, do you?'

'Are you saying you believe Jerusalem's spirit is in the house?' Bartholomew asked. 'I've never performed an exorcism, but I believe there are priests who can.'

'I'm not saying I don't believe it, exactly,' Francis said at the same time. 'But I do agree with Amias. It does seem rather far-fetched.'

'I once saw a ghost,' Constance was

mumbling. 'I've kept it to myself because, well, one doesn't discuss such things. Especially a vicar's wife. But Mary could be right.'

Mary banged her fist on the table. 'Can we please all not speak at once! And stop talking about ghosts. I won't get a wink of sleep tonight.'

'I don't think any of us will.' Cat leant towards Amias and he wrapped an arm around her shoulder.

'I know that if a body, or even a skeleton, is found anywhere,' Francis said, when everyone fell silent for a second, 'the police must be informed. They need to decide whether it's 'a forensic case of interest to the police', I believe the term is. And whether or not it will form part of a criminal investigation. To do that, they need to date it, and determine whether or not a crime was committed.'

'If Jerusalem really is under that floor,' Amias said. 'I think we can all safely assume she didn't get there by herself. And there is this confession. However garbled it may be.'

'Yes. But if the body is found to be centuries old, it's classed as being 'bones of antiquity' and the police would no longer be involved. I'm not sure what would happen in a case like this, but I am sure we need to inform them.'

Amias nodded. 'I've got friends in the local police. I can give them a call and see where we go from here.'

'I'm going as far away from here as possible,' Mary said. 'And if that poor young woman is under that floor, I'm going to have to sell this house. I can't live here knowing that something like this has happened beneath my larder. I don't think I can ever go in there again.'

Chapter Fourteen

Francis was right about the police.

Amias called one of his friends at the Merriment Bay Police Station and put him on speaker phone, explaining how they'd found the cellar and the coffer and that they thought there might be a body of a woman beneath the cellar floor.

'Are you having me on, mate?'

'No,' Amias said. 'We don't know if there is a body but we want to know what would happen if there was.' He told his friend about the confession. 'The ink's faded and some of the writing is illegible but it's definitely a confession and the start of the name George is clear, as is the name Devon. We can't read the two middle names in between them, but we know that a George Devon lived here at the time and we also know he was a justice of the peace and the one Jerusalem's disappearance, and the so-called theft of the painting would've been reported to. So it seems the case against Titus was a complete and utter stitch-up, but whether George acted alone or whether his friends or anyone else was involved, we'll probably never know. At least there's one thing we do know, if this is genuine, that is. Titus Wells didn't steal the painting and he didn't murder Jerusalem. What is now a mystery, is whether this George Devon, did, and whether he buried her in the hidden cellar or if this is all some sort of weird and terrible prank. And there's only one way we'll find out.'

'Blow me down. I've never come across anything like this. I'm sorry about Titus, and there's nothing much I can say or do about that, but if someone finds a body, or has reason to suspect they know where a body is, we would contact the CID. That's the Criminal Investigation Department. They'd make an initial and brief assessment. Then the site would be sealed off and a crime scene manager, along with a specialist forensic team would carry out examinations to establish the circumstances. Photos would be taken and if necessary, additional experts called in. But we'd only be further involved if the bones were from recent times and it was possible to investigate the crime. Two hundred years ago isn't classed as recent. Although to be honest, I'm not certain where the cut-off point is. Not something I'd expect to have to deal with here in Merriment Bay. But I do know that, pursuant to the Burial Act of 1857, human remains can only be exhumed by someone with a licence to do so and that all human remains must be reported to the Coroner's Office. So you can't just dig her up if she is there. Bones of antiquity fall under the remit of the county archaeologist, I believe, but they're usually only interested in ancient bones of historical interest. If it is Jerusalem Raine, her body will probably be released to her family for burial. Although there may be an inquest. That's for the coroner to decide.'

Amias looked around the table. 'Then I suppose we need to report that we believe there may be a body beneath the cellar floor in Devon Villa.'

'Right you are. I'll send someone round to take a look and get some details and I'll pass the information on to the CID. And Amias. This'll probably get into the papers. You know that, don't you? There's nothing we can do to stop that.'

'The papers?' Mary squealed. 'How can this be happening?'

Chapter Fifteen

Mary flatly refused to spend another moment in Devon Villa once the police arrived and went down into the cellar. Constance and Bartholomew Raine kindly suggested that she should spend that night at least, at the rectory with them. But Mary had other ideas and immediately phoned Gladys who was happy for Mary to stay with her and her daughter Lorna for as long as Mary liked.

'Why don't you come and stay at Amias'?' Cat asked, somewhat surprised by Mary's decision. 'That's where Kyra and I will be staying until the police have finished here.'

'Perhaps I will in a day or two. But for tonight at least, I really feel I would rather stay with Gladys. She suffers from insomnia, so we'll be able to keep one another occupied playing cards throughout the night. I need to do something to take my mind off this dreadful business and I know for a fact that I won't be able to sleep.'

Cat was reluctant to let Mary go, but Amias persuaded her it might be for the best.

'Just for tonight,' he said. 'We can review the situation tomorrow when we have a better idea of what's happening here. Why don't you and Kyra leave this to me and Francis to deal with, and go back to our place to get some rest? You look worn out.'

'I won't be able to sleep either. But I would like to get out of here, if that's really all right with you and Francis?'

'It's fine by me,' Francis said. 'They only want to ask me some questions about the painting, Jerusalem's story, and this confession, and how I found it.'

Amias nodded. 'And they want to ask me about finding the painting. So there's really no need for you to stay.'

'What about me?' Kyra asked. 'I was with Francis when he found the confession.'

'I think if you just tell them that, then you'll be free to go. Francis can tell them everything else they need to know. And it's not as if there's going to be a criminal investigation, because as my friend said, there's no one left alive to prosecute. If anything, it'll just be an inquest. And we can deal with that if and when it happens.'

Kyra yawned. 'I am pretty tired. I could definitely do with some sleep. Come on Mum.

Let's leave them to it.'

'OK. I'll call for cabs to take us all to our various destinations. Will you help Mum pack some things? And pack some for yourself. I've already got a few bits at Amias', so I don't need anything for now. Oh. But I'd better clear up the dinner plates and load the dishwasher before I go.'

'We can help with that,' Constance said.

'Thanks. But it'll only take a moment. May I ask you and Bartholomew to accompany Mum in a cab to make sure she arrives safely at Gladys', if you don't mind?'

'Not at all,' Bartholomew said. 'We'll make sure she's safely inside before we go on our way.'

'I can manage perfectly well,' Mary said, somewhat indignantly.

'I know, Mum. But I'd be happier if you'd go with them.'

'Oh very well. I'll call you in the morning. Thank you, Amias for staying behind. And you too, Francis. I expect you think I'm a foolish old woman, but on top of everything else that's happened recently, I'm afraid this has hit me rather harder than I might have expected.'

'We understand completely.' Amias placed a hand on Mary's shoulder. 'And you're not old, Mary. And you're definitely not foolish.'

She smiled up at him and to everyone's surprise, kissed him on the cheek.

'It's astonishing how wrong someone can be about another person, Amias, and I'm sorry for the way I've behaved towards you in the past.'

'Don't give it another thought, Mary.'

'Thank you,' she said, letting out a sigh. 'I wish to God I had learnt that lesson before I met Jeremy Stone. I rather hope that one day, someone buries him in their cellar.'

'Don't dwell on Jeremy now, Mum.' Cat gave Mary a hug and a kiss and dialled the number for the cab office.

'You go too,' Amias said. 'I'm sure Francis won't mind helping me load the dishwasher.'

Francis smiled. 'I can do that.' Then he looked at Kyra. 'Would you like a hand carrying down the bags?'

Kyra hesitated for a second before smiling and shaking her head. 'No thanks. I'm not planning to take that much, and I can manage Gran's bag. I heard what the police said to Amias when they arrived. This shouldn't take more than a few days, and then we'll be allowed to come and go. If it is Jerusalem, they won't need to cordon off the house. Only the larder and the cellar will be out of bounds until they've removed her.'

'And possibly the kitchen,' Francis added.

Kyra nodded. 'I bet you didn't expect tonight to end like this.'

'You're right. I didn't. Although from the

moment I saw you standing on that corner, I had a feeling the evening was going to be anything but ordinary.'

'Oh. That reminds me.' She took the ten-pound note he'd given her earlier, out of her pocket and held it out to him. 'This belongs to you.'

He grinned. 'Keep it. You can buy me a cup of coffee sometime over the weekend. I'll be at the rectory till Monday morning.' He handed her what looked like a business card.

'Deal.' She took it, turned and raced towards the stairs.

'And if you need a coat,' he added. 'I'll see you at the church at 2 p.m. tomorrow.'

She glanced over her shoulder and grinned. 'A girl can never have too many coats.'

'You've got plenty of coats,' Cat said, completely bemused by their conversation.

They simply smiled at her and at one another, and Kyra continued up the stairs.

Cat had no intention of leaving the matter there. Ever since Francis had arrived, there had been something strange going on between him and Kyra. There was definitely some sort of chemistry between them.

'Not quite how you imagined spending this weekend, eh, Francis?'

He dragged his gaze from Kyra's back and followed Cat into the dining room.

'Not quite. Although I was going to be

digging up more of Jerusalem's history, so in a way, it is. I just wasn't expecting, in a million years, that I'd be involved in digging up her body.'

'No. I don't think many of us saw that coming. Apart from, maybe, Mum, and possibly Kyra.' Cat stacked the plates on a tray while Francis did the same with the glasses and coffee cups and saucers. 'Do you have a girlfriend in London?'

'A girlfriend?' He sounded surprised but he smiled. 'No. I've got some female friends, but there's no one special.'

'That's a shame.' Cat took the tray to the kitchen with Francis right behind her. 'Kyra's got a boyfriend. His name's Lucas. He couldn't be here tonight because he's out with some male friends on a sort of stag night for one of them.'

'Yes. She told me about him.'

'She did? That's good. Lucas is a lovely young man. Kyra was supposed to be going to university but she deferred her place last year because ... of family matters. She and Lucas started dating almost from the day they met. If things between them continue as they are, the pair of them may go travelling this summer and then she'll start uni in September. In Edinburgh. It's a long way from here, but she has such a bright future ahead of her.' Cat met his gaze as she put her tray on the worktop above the dishwasher. 'I have no idea why I told you all that.'

Francis gave her a crooked smile and put his tray beside hers.

'Don't you? I think I do.'

'Catherine! The cabs are here.' Mary appeared in the doorway.

'Leave this with me,' Francis said. 'Everything's in safe hands.'

Cat smiled at him. Was he talking about the glasses and crockery? Or something else entirely? She wasn't completely sure. But she was sure about the look on Kyra's face when Kyra popped her head into the kitchen a second later.

'We're going now, Francis. It was lovely to meet you.'

'Same here,' he replied.

'I'll see you tomorrow?' She sounded as if she wanted confirmation.

'Maybe.'

'Maybe?'

'Come along sweetheart,' Cat said, linking her arm through Kyra's. 'We mustn't keep Mum and the cabs waiting. Goodbye, Francis.'

'Bye for now,' Francis said.

Cat led Kyra towards the front door, stopping briefly to give Amias a quick kiss. She made sure Mary, Constance and Bartholomew got into their cab before getting into the cab for her and Kyra.

'What was all that business with you and Francis?' Cat asked, as their cab headed towards Amias' house.

'What business?'

'About the coat. And the money you offered him. And the fact you seemed to loiter in the hall for quite some time when he arrived. Not to mention the fact that you appeared to be very keen to arrange to see him again.'

'Oh Mum. It was just a little joke between us.'

'What sort of joke?'

'Does it matter?'

'It might matter to Lucas.'

Kyra twisted in her seat and stared at Cat. 'What does that mean?'

Cat sighed wearily. 'It means that I saw the way the two of you looked at one another, especially during dinner. You only met the man tonight. And he's ten years older than you. He's handsome and he's clearly very bright. He's also very nice. But do you really want to risk what you have with Lucas for a little flirtation over a weekend?'

'Mum!' Kyra glowered at her. 'Can't I laugh and joke with another man without being accused of flirting?'

'Of course you can. But you were definitely flirting. Remember what you said to me at Christmas when I didn't know what was going on with Amias, or with Ben? You accused me of

135

leading them on. Well, I hate to say this, sweetheart. But you were definitely leading Francis on tonight.'

Kyra opened her mouth to speak but shut it again and glanced out of the cab window for a moment or two.

'I'm sorry, Mum.' She looked Cat directly in the eye. 'I do remember that. And you're right. But here's the thing. Do you remember telling me that you loved Dad, but that you also loved Amias?'

'Of course I do. Oh Kyra. No. Surely not? You've only known Francis for a few hours.'

Kyra nodded. 'True. But didn't you also tell me that you fell in love with Amias the minute you saw him? I'm not saying I did that with Francis. I'm not even saying I love him. Because I don't. I definitely do not. But it's weird. When I saw him running along Coast Road towards me tonight, I felt something. I don't know what. I honestly don't. But it was definitely something. And when he thought I was a hooker, he was so kind and caring and that really tugged at my heart.'

Cat stared at her, open mouthed. 'When he thought you were a what?'

Kyra laughed. 'I'll tell you about it over a cup of hot chocolate when we get to Amias.'

'I can't wait.' She didn't bother to hide the sarcasm. 'There's nothing a mother likes to hear more than that a young man thinks her daughter is a prostitute.'

Kyra laughed louder. 'It was actually pretty funny. He really made me laugh. I think we've got the same sense of humour.'

'Yes. Well be careful, sweetheart. Don't go down a path unless you're sure you're prepared to face what you find at the end of it. And don't go chasing moonbeams.'

'Chasing moonbeams?' Kyra sniggered.

'Oh dear God.' Cat shook her head before grinning at Kyra. 'I've turned into a combination of Mum and Granny Viola. I'm giving you unwanted advice based on my feelings, not yours. And 'chasing moonbeams' is a phrase Granny Viola often used. Please kill me now.'

Kyra laughed. 'I think one dead body is quite enough for tonight.' She sat back against the seat and sighed. 'Chasing moonbeams. I like that. There's something mystical and magical about it. I wonder if that's why Jerusalem called her painting, *Moonbeams Kiss*. Because she and Titus were in love and they both knew they were chasing moonbeams. They knew they could never be together.'

'Possibly. It's all very sad.'

'It's unfair. And it's wrong. Why do so many people who are in love, have to spend their lives apart? Jerusalem and Titus. Viola and Bailey. Even you and Amias. Although you two finally got together. But you spent so many years apart. I'll tell you one thing right now, Mum. When I'm in love. I mean really in love. I'll move heaven and earth to make sure I can be with the man I love. Assuming he feels the same, that is. I won't let anything keep us apart. I won't let love slip through my fingers, or let my chance for happiness slip away.'

'Good for you, Kyra. I'm very pleased to hear that. But you're young and you've got your entire life ahead of you. You might fall in love more than once. You may be in love several times. And sometimes you will think you're in love when you're not. Or you may fall for the wrong man. Sometimes love plays tricks on people. Look at Mum and Jeremy. Just make sure the love you fight for is worth it.' Cat sighed. 'And there's Granny Viola speaking, yet again.'

'I really wish I'd been able to spend a little time with Granny Viola. That's another thing. We never know how long we've got. Take Great Aunt Ivy for example. She thought she had her entire life ahead of her, and then she flew her plane into a hillside and died. I'm going to live my life as if each day may be my last.'

'Oh good. That's a cheery note. I think.'

'I'm going to grab every opportunity that comes my way. And if I do fall in love with someone, I'm going to tell them. I'm not going to wait eighteen years to find out if they feel the same. Sorry, Mum. That's not a criticism of you and Amias.'

'I agree with you, sweetheart. Amias and I wasted such a lot of time. If only one of us had had the courage to speak out, we might have been together all those years ago. If you love someone, and I mean really love them, you should definitely tell them. Even if they don't feel the same, all you'll lose by saying it is a little bit of pride.'

'That doesn't bother me. We Devon women are strong, as Gran is always saying. We can take rejection.'

The cab pulled up outside Amias' and Cat and Kyra got out.

'Look at the moon, Mum.'

Kyra pointed heavenward and Cat looked up. The moon had a kind of halo around it. A ghostly ring. Cat shivered as she looked at it.

'It's beautiful. Although Granny Viola would say that it's a warning. A foretelling of bad things to come.'

Kyra grinned at her. 'Seriously? It's caused by ice particles. And the only thing it foretells is that rain might be on the way, if I remember correctly. But it does seem strange given what's happened tonight, doesn't it? Or am I also turning into a younger version of Granny Viola?'

'God forbid.'

Kyra pulled out her phone and took a photo. 'I'm going to send this to Francis and tell him that it's a sign that Jerusalem is happy that we've found her and that she's finally with Titus. Assuming we have found her. You know? Like that double rainbow we all saw on the day of Granny Viola and Bailey's funeral.'

Her thumbs raced across the screen and her phone pinged as the message was sent.

Cat took a deep breath. 'You've got Francis' phone number? And he's the only person you think of to send the photo of the moon? Not to your gran, to help her feel a little better about the possibility of finding Jerusalem's body in her cellar? I think the only sign here is the one that you may be interested in someone other than your boyfriend.'

'He gave it to me in case I wanted to get in touch about meeting him for coffee this weekend.' Kyra looked her in the eye and held her gaze, until Kyra's phone pinged back to notify a reply. Kyra darted an excited look at the screen. 'He says that Love will always find a way, no matter how long it takes. Oh God, Mum. I think perhaps you're right. I may be just a teensy tiny bit interested in Francis Raine.'

Chapter Sixteen

Cat had no idea how they were going to get through all of this, but she was thankful to be kept busy. When Constance Raine and Abigail Lester both called her via video chat the following morning, to ask if she, Kyra and Mary would step in to help organise the annual dance for Valentine's Day – the Merriment Bay Moonlight Valentine's Dance, Cat jumped at the chance. Apparently one or two of the members of the W.I. who were on the events committee, had fallen ill and needed to be replaced.

'We'd love to,' Cat told both Constance and Abigail, without bothering to check with Kyra or with Mary.

Luckily for Cat, Kyra agreed immediately when Cat broached the subject a little later that morning. Cat had brought Mary back to Amias' house for coffee, and to show her the bedroom in which Amias had said that Mary could stay, if she wanted.

Mary took a little persuasion. On both counts.

'The bedroom is beautiful. And not at all what I'd expected to find in Amias' house. In fact, the entire house is beautiful, I'm somewhat surprised to say. But Gladys and Lorna are happy for me to stay with them and I really think I might be in the way if I stayed here.'

'You won't, Mum. It's a decent sized house. We won't get under one another's feet.'

'It's not our feet that concerns me. I'm astonished to find that I'm actually growing to like Amias more each day, although his D.I.Y skills leave a lot to be desired. But he's a kind and caring man and I can see why you're in love with him. The thing is, I'm not sure he really wants me living here. And I completely understand. No young couple wants an elderly parent living with them.'

'Stop right there. You're not elderly, Mum. And if he didn't want you living here, he'd say so. He may have had trouble telling me he loved me, but he's never had a problem with telling people he doesn't like them. However nicely he may phrase it.'

'He's only invited me because he wants to make you happy.'

'He's invited you because he cares. You may not believe this, but it was his suggestion, not mine. And he's worried about you. He told me last night that he'd rather you were here so that if you felt upset at all, you would have us all close by. And he included himself in that. He actually likes you. That came as a surprise to me too, but he genuinely does.'

'Did he say that?'

Cat nodded. 'He said he's grown surprisingly fond of you and he wants to make sure you're OK.'

'Well in that case, I will stay. But not tonight. I promised Gladys and Lorna that we'd have another game of bridge tonight. Annie is joining us. I'll come and stay from tomorrow, if the offer is still open by then.'

'Of course it is. You're welcome here whenever you want. So now that matter is settled, what about the Merriment Bay Moonlight Valentine's Dance?'

'What about it? I really don't want to get involved.'

'It'll help to distract us from what's happening at Devon Villa, Mum.'

'It may help you and Kyra, Catherine, but sitting around a table with Constance and Abigail, and all the rest of the W.I. discussing bunting and music and buffets and such, isn't my idea of a distraction. In fact, it's an added torment.'

'It might be fun,' Kyra said.

'It won't.'

Cat grinned. 'I'll take some wine and nibbles and we'll make it more like a girl's get together.'

Mary raised her brows and stared at Cat.

'A girl's get together? With Constance Raine? I like the woman, don't misunderstand me. But I spent last night in her company, and one evening a week is more than enough time to spend with Constance, let me assure you.'

'Don't be a misery, Gran.' Kyra gave her a playful nudge. 'Didn't you say you were going to be open to new experiences from now on?'

'I don't think anyone would call me a misery. Well. Perhaps one or two people might. But that's not important. I don't recall using those words. I believe I said that we should all live life to the full. Organising the Merriment Bay Moonlight Valentine's Dance is not, exactly, living life to the full.'

'But it's a start, Gran. And if we're involved in organising the dance, at least we'll be able to make sure that the food and music are to our liking.'

Mary smiled. 'You do have a point there, darling. Oh all right. I'll help.'

Having got Mary on board with that, Kyra said she had to go.

'I'm meeting Francis for coffee.'

'Now?' Cat glanced at her watch. 'It's only 11 and I thought you mentioned something about meeting at 2 at St. Mary-in-the-Fields?'

'We did. But that was really a joke. Because of the coat thing. He sent me a text just after nine, asking if I wanted to meet up earlier. I don't need a coat but I do need coffee.'

'He seems rather keen.' Mary raised her brows and smiled.

'You've just had coffee,' Cat said.

'I need more coffee, Mum.'

'Hmm.' Mary gave her a playful slap as Kyra kissed her on the cheek. 'You need to have coffee with a handsome young man, you mean, and not with your mother and your gran. Or your boyfriend, come to that.'

Kyra tutted and kissed Cat. 'I love you both, but yes. I'll admit it. I do want to have coffee with Francis. Don't look at me like that, Mum. I'll be careful and I promise I won't do anything I shouldn't.'

'What about Francis? He might.'

'I don't think he would. He was flirting with me yesterday, that's true. But I don't think he'd take it any further. Sadly.'

'Kyra!'

'I was teasing. I wouldn't do anything behind Lucas' back. But in a way I think it'll be good for me to see Francis again. I want to know if I really do like him or if it was all just the excitement of last night. If I'm having doubts about my relationship with Lucas, isn't it better we both find out now?'

'I suppose that's true.'

Cat understood how Kyra felt but she hoped Kyra's feelings for Lucas would prevail.

'Are you having doubts?' Mary asked, as Kyra headed towards the door.

'One or two. I'll see you later. Have fun. And don't find any bodies while I'm gone.'

Mary shook her head. 'Sometimes I worry about that child. She is so much like you, that's it's rather concerning.'

'Really? I think she takes after Kyle far more than she does me. She's definitely got his brains.'

'Let's hope she uses them. Because she's definitely got your heart. And we all know where that led you. Although having said that, Kyle was the one who wanted to run away, wasn't he? He put that foolish notion in your head then lied about it to Amias and said it was you who wanted to run away. But anyway, that obviously makes things worse. Kyra takes after both of you.'

'Mum! Kyra is not going to run off with Francis Raine.'

'I didn't say she was. I'm simply pointing out that where love is concerned, Kyra may not always make the wisest choices. Let's be honest, darling. Have any of the Devon women? And before you tell me that Amias is a wise choice, I fully accept that. But perhaps Kyle wasn't. Although without Kyle, you wouldn't have Kyra. But then again, if you'd told Amias how you felt about him all those years ago, you and he would be married with children of your own right now. Isn't that a sobering thought?'

It was. And one that strangely enough, made Cat feel angry.

'If you and Granny Viola hadn't been such bloody snobs, or thought you both knew what was best for me, and interfered in all our lives, perhaps none of us would have got into the situations in which we found ourselves.'

Mary coughed. 'Yes. Well. I thought we'd all agreed to let go of the past. I shouldn't have mentioned it.'

'No, Mum. You shouldn't.'

Silence hung between them for a moment or two.

'There's still time you know, my darling.' Mary's voice was tender and loving and she reached out and squeezed Cat's hand.

'Time? Time for what?'

'For you and Amias to have a child.'

Cat's mouth dropped open and she stared at her mum.

Sometimes Mary made Cat so cross.

Especially when the woman seemed to be able to read her mind.

Chapter Seventeen

Cat had also contacted Rafe on that Friday morning, before she had gone to pick up Mary to bring her back for coffee. She called to tell him and Adam all about the cellar and the confession in the coffer and that the police were now at Devon Villa waiting for the specialists to arrive and start digging up the cellar floor. She thought it might make her new-found family think twice about making their relationship to her and Kyra, public, but if anything, it made them more determined to announce it to the world. Although they were as stunned as she expected them to be about Jerusalem Raine.

'I'm not sure what to say,' Rafe said, 'and clearly nor is Adam.' He'd already told her that he and Adam were together in his study and he'd put her call on speaker-phone. 'Are you and Kyra OK?'

'We're fine, thanks. Mum's more upset

than us.'

'I expect she is,' Adam said. 'I'm not sure I'd like to know that I'd been living my entire life in a house with a body buried in the cellar.'

'Come to Sunday lunch,' Rafe said, 'we can discuss it properly and decide the best course of action. But please call us beforehand if you need anything at all, won't you, Cat?'

'Sunday lunch?' That was a surprise. 'Kyra and me?'

'And Amias, of course. And Mary, if she feels up to it. If she's upset, she may not want to come to Wynter House. I don't believe our father would have brought her here, but the place may hold unsettling memories for her.'

'It might. But I think she'd like to join us. If you're both sure that's OK.'

'We're sure,' said Adam.

'And Olivia? Will she be OK with us all being there? Especially Mum.'

There was a momentary silence.

'To be honest,' Rafe said. 'Olivia is spending most of her time in her own rooms. She doesn't seem to enjoy company since her heart attack. I hope she'll want to join us, but please don't take it personally if she doesn't. There's plenty of time for you to meet her.'

That sounded as if he was fairly certain she wouldn't be meeting Olivia for the foreseeable future. But in a way, she was rather glad about that. What with everything else going on, meeting Olivia Wynter could definitely wait.

And on Sunday morning, as Amias drove her, Kyra and Mary along the tree-lined drive to Wynter House, she sincerely hoped she wouldn't be meeting Olivia that day. The house was intimidating enough. The immense size of the place was the first thing that struck her, but it was the sheer beauty of the red brick façade, consisting of two protruding square towers topped with onion-shaped, lead roofs, either side of a large central portion that took her breath away. Light bounced off the mullioned windows and the lead glistened in the pale sunlight.

Mary gave a loud gasp as the house came into view and Kyra gave a long, low whistle.

'Bloody hell, Mum. Are we really related to the owners of this place?'

Cat nodded. 'I expected it to be a large house, but I never expected it to be this grand. Haven't you ever been here, Mum?' She glanced at Mary who was in the back seat sitting next to Kyra.

'No. Your father never invited me. For obvious reasons. After his death, we knew we were even less welcome. When Rafe opened the place to paying visitors, Mother and I did discuss coming on one of the tours. But we decided it was best not to step into that particular puddle. "You'll be chasing moonbeams, Mary", Mother told me. And I thought she was right. I still can't believe we've been invited here for lunch. I wonder what Olivia will have to say about this.'

'I have a feeling we won't get to find out. Rafe told me that she keeps herself to herself these days.'

She was right. Olivia felt too unwell to join them. A fact that didn't seem to please either Rafe or Adam as they welcomed their guests, but that definitely pleased Neva, although she did say it was a pity Cat and Kyra wouldn't get to meet their grandmother and great-grandmother, respectively.

'This house is so beautiful,' Cat said, trying not to sound too emotional.

'This house is also your home,' Rafe said, smiling at Cat and Kyra. 'You're welcome here at any time, whether it's for a brief visit, or to come here to stay. Wynter House is, and always will be, home to the Wynter family. And to their loved ones, of course.' He smiled at Amias and Mary.

'Wow!' Kyra said. 'I might take you up on that one day.'

'Please do,' Rafe said, and he looked completely genuine.

'He means that,' Adam added. 'As do I. You are family, and Wynter House is your ancestral home.'

'You might not want us here when all this latest stuff comes out and everyone in

Merriment Bay starts gossiping. Or if there are reporters banging on your door,' Cat said.

Adam grinned. 'I hate to say this, but you're the ones who'll be bearing the brunt of most of the gossip now that the body of Jerusalem Raine has been found in your cellar.'

'We may need somewhere to hide out from the press,' Kyra said, laughing. 'I like the thought of having an ancestral home to run to.'

Rafe laughed. 'This is the perfect place to do that. They can't set foot on the drive, and if they do, Carruthers here will soon show them the error of their ways, won't you, Archie?'

Carruthers, the butler, had been standing to one side, as if to attention, and Cat only spotted him when Rafe held out his hand and called the man over. He wore formal dress of a white, wing collar dress shirt, black morning coat and matching tie, grey waistcoat and grey, pinstriped trousers. He also wore white gloves and he gave a slight bow as Rafe introduced him.

'I most certainly shall, Mr Rafe,' Carruthers said, raising one eyebrow and lowering the other.

Adam laughed. 'Excuse the formal attire. Olivia insisted on it. Carruthers is usually a little more casual. Although not much. Olivia believes in all the pomp, but even Carruthers believes there are certain standards to uphold. Don't you?'

Adam patted the butler on the shoulder and Carruthers gave a small smile as his eyebrows rose and fell once again.

'Indeed there are, Mr Adam. It's an honour to meet you, Miss Catherine and Miss Kyra.' He gave them both a little bow of his head.

'We're delighted to meet you,' Cat said. 'But please just call us, Cat and Kyra.'

Neva laughed. 'Good luck with that. Sorry, Carruthers. I'm not making fun of you.' She beamed at him and he gave her a faint smile and a nod.

'Let's have some drinks,' Adam said, wrapping his arm around his girlfriend, Hazel's waist. 'I'm dying to hear all about Jerusalem Raine and how you came to find her body in your cellar.'

'Please don't remind us of that,' Mary said. 'I'm definitely going to have to sell the house.'

'Because of the body in the cellar?' Neva asked.

'Yes. But it's not only because of this latest tragedy. It just doesn't feel the same now that Mother's gone. And everywhere I look I'm reminded of Jeremy Stone, mainly due to the fact that all the work he started has been left unfinished, and my en suite is more like a building site than a place of sanctuary. Oh! I'm sorry. I have no idea why I brought that up.'

'I happen to know a good builder,' Neva suggested, with a comforting smile. 'And he happens to live next door to you.'

Mary smiled in return. 'Dennis is wonderful, and I must confess, Catherine, Kyra and I have already discussed that possibility, but only briefly, what with all this going on. And we may need to avail ourselves of his services in order to sell, but even if the place was refurbished from the gables to the foundations, I will never come to terms with there having been a body in my cellar, or the fact that my mother no longer walks the rooms.'

'Will you buy somewhere else, or are you intending to stay with Cat and Amias?' Neva asked.

Amias' face dropped but he soon recovered himself. 'You can stay with us for as long as you like, Mary. Although having been used to living in such a large house as Devon Villa, mine may start to feel a little cramped to you, with the four of us living there. Not that there isn't plenty of room for us all.'

Mary grinned at him. 'Don't worry, Amias. The very same thought had already crossed my mind. There's a bungalow coming up for sale two doors away from Gladys. Old Jacob was going to be moving into an old people's home around Easter time, so it was going to be on the market sooner or later, but he sadly passed away yesterday. I may put in an offer for that. I was planning on visiting Natalia and Josh this week to discuss it. Horton and Wells can sell my house, and I can buy Jacob's bungalow. I'll have to hope that the gruesome discovery in the cellar doesn't put off potential buyers.'

'If you're really serious about selling Devon Villa,' Neva said, beaming with excitement, 'I may know someone who'll be interested to buy. Sorry to do your sister out of the commission, Amias. But we're hoping my sister Rowan and her family will move to Merriment Bay. They've said they'd like to but suitable properties are few and far between. Devon Villa would be the perfect house for them. Nigel's a builder. Rowan loves Edwardian houses. Finding a body in the cellar won't bother them. It'll be an added attraction as far as my niece, Sasha is concerned. I know they'll make you a really good offer.'

Cat smiled at Mary. 'It seems that everything may work out well for quite a few of us. Although I do want you to give this some very serious thought, Mum. You've lived in Devon Villa all your life. Selling up shouldn't be done lightly. It'll be a big upheaval.'

'Change is often the best medicine, so they say,' Mary said. 'Perhaps it's time I put the past behind me and went in search of my new future. After all, isn't that what most of us here are doing? You and your long-lost family. And you and Amias. Kyra and ... well, Kyra and wherever and with whomsoever she decides her future may lie. Rafe and Neva. Adam and Hazel. Dennis and Dawn's move. Not forgetting Annie and Alwick, although that's still early days. But my point is, so many people are starting afresh. Why shouldn't I be one of them?'

Chapter Eighteen

Cat was pleased when that first weekend was over. She was thrilled that she'd been to Wynter House. Delighted to have spent so much time on Sunday with her brothers and their girlfriends. Pleased to have met all the guests from the village who were staying at the house. Both disappointed and relieved not to have had a chance to meet Olivia Wynter. But most of all, she was happy that Kyra hadn't made any drastic decisions about either Francis, or her relationship with Lucas.

Cat knew her pleasure on that score would be short-lived. Francis had told Kyra he intended to return to the rectory the following weekend, just, he said, to keep up to date with what was happening regarding Jerusalem. But on Wednesday, he called and invited them all to the rectory for dinner on Friday night. Kyra had put him on loud speaker.

'Oh. I was going to ask if you could come

round here for Sunday lunch,' Kyra suddenly announced.

'We could do both,' Amias suggested, smiling at Cat as if he thought she would love the idea.

'That sounds great,' Francis said, and Kyra, of course, agreed.

'I'll take you for a private tour of the museum if you like,' Amias added.

'Wow! Yes please.' Francis sounded genuinely excited.

'Haven't you been to the museum?' Cat asked.

'Once or twice, over the years. But I've never had a private tour and it would be much more interesting with a guide who really knows his stuff. Would it be possible to take a look at your Spitfire?'

'Of course,' Amias said.

'Am I invited on this tour?' Kyra asked.

Cat felt on edge. Kyra hadn't shown much interest in the place once Amias had traced Bailey Mitchell, back in December. Was it simply because Francis would be going?

'Absolutely,' Amias said.

No one made any mention of Lucas.

'Are we inviting Lucas too?' Cat tried to sound calm and indifferent. As if it wasn't a big deal.

'He's going away for the weekend,' Kyra said. 'He's going up to Oxford to spend some time alone with Marcus. I thought I'd mentioned it.'

'You hadn't,' Cat said.

Kyra shrugged. 'Oh well. He is. So he won't be coming to lunch on Sunday.'

'I was going to say you were welcome to bring him with you to the rectory on Friday night,' Francis said. And he sounded sincere.

'Thanks. But he's travelling up to Oxford on Friday afternoon.'

'That's a shame.'

'Is it?' Kyra sounded surprised.

'Yes. I'd like to have met him. Another time, perhaps.'

'We'll see you on Friday evening then,' Amias said, as Kyra wandered towards the door with her phone – and with Francis still on loud speaker.

'Bye for now,' Francis replied.

'Don't ring off.' Kyra glanced over her shoulder at Cat and Amias. 'I want to talk to you about Jerusalem and Titus.'

'Sorry, Kyra. I've got to go. There's another call waiting and it's one I really need to take. I can call you back later, but it may not be until this evening.'

'Don't bother. I'll talk to you on Friday. You're clearly far too busy.' She hung up and marched into the hall.

'Am I imagining it, or does Kyra have a thing for Francis?' Amias furrowed his brows.

Cat tutted. 'She's had a thing for him since the first evening they met. Why did you have to invite him for Sunday lunch?'

'I like him. I thought you liked him too.'

'I do. He's a lovely guy. The problem is that Kyra likes him, and she shouldn't.'

'Shouldn't? I know she's dating Lucas, and I'd hate to see him get hurt, but please don't tell me you're going to start interfering in your daughter's love life, Cat. We both know to our cost where that can lead.'

'Don't look at me like that. She's my daughter and I worry about her, that's all. I can't help it.'

'Of course you do. I worry about her too. But she's eighteen, Cat and she needs to make her own choices and her own mistakes. Hopefully she won't make too many. She's a bright kid.'

Cat sighed. That was exactly what Cat believed and had always said she would do. Until now.

'But Francis is twenty-eight.'

'And?'

'She's eighteen.'

He nodded. 'Yes. So what? A ten-year age difference is nothing. And Kyra's fairly mature for her age.'

'That's one of the things that worries me.'

He walked to her and wrapped her in his arms.

'She needs to spread her wings, Cat. And you need to let her. You know that. If you try to clip them, all you'll get is someone wondering if they could ever fly. If you let her try, she might reach the moon and bring you back some stardust.' He laughed. 'I'm not sure if that made sense, or even where that came from. I think I'm spending too much time with your mother.'

Cat laughed too. 'It made a lot of sense. You're right. Not about spending too much time with Mum. I mean about Kyra. I'll let her fly. I always said I would. If you hear me lecturing her or sticking my nose in, please tell me. I'll give her my advice but I mustn't tell her what she should or shouldn't do.'

'I'll tell you if I think you sound like Mary and Viola. Where is your mum, by the way?'

'Having coffee with Gladys and Annie. And I think she's popping in to see Natalia. She wants to arrange to view that bungalow she mentioned.'

'She's seriously thinking of moving out?'

Cat smiled up at him and nodded.

'Try not to sound quite so pleased about that prospect when Mum mentions it again.' She kissed him on the lips. 'Now I really need to go. I promised Abigail I'd pop round to discuss balloons for the Merriment Bay Moonlight Valentine's Dance.'

'And I must go and meet Will. I promised

161

him we'd have a pint and see where we are with our lists.'

Amias, and Will Lester, who jointly owned the museum had celebrations of their own to organise while Cat, Kyra and Mary were helping out with organising the Merriment Bay Moonlight Valentine's Dance.

This year marked the 75th anniversary of VE Day on the 8th of May and also the 80th anniversary of the Battle of Britain on the 15th of September, although the battle itself lasted from early July until the end of October, 1940.

The government had already announced plans for the May celebrations, including moving the annual Early May Bank Holiday from the Monday to the following Friday, something that hadn't pleased every member of the British public, when it was announced.

There would be several events in London, including a Red Arrows Display and a Battle of Britain Memorial Flight. St James's Park was to be transformed into Victory Park with examples of life in Britain during the war, and Winston Churchill's famous Victory speech was to be broadcast in public places throughout the country. In addition, pubs, clubs and cinemas were all being allowed to stay open into the early hours.

So far, the Mayor of Merriment Bay, who also happened to be Will Lester, had announced a VE Day celebration on the common, including stalls selling goods and memorabilia relating to the 1940s, all day music, followed by a dance in the evening along with silent fireworks. Amias would fly his Spitfire over the village and there was a competition to win a passenger-flight in his plane. Tickets were already selling faster than expected for that.

Lucas was also helping his dad and Amias with the celebrations, as was his cousin Marcus, who would be returning to Merriment Bay from Oxford uni for part of the summer holidays. According to Kyra, Lucas and Marcus were constantly face-timing one another, with ideas, or playing computer games, neither of which Kyra had much interest in.

But Kyra did seem to have found an interest of her own – apart from Francis Raine. She'd become fascinated with Jerusalem Raine and Titus Wells and was determined to discover as much as she could about both. She also wanted to find out all she could about George Devon and why he might have wanted to murder poor Jerusalem. Kyra spent a great deal of time doing research; some of it with Francis, with whom she frequently chatted on line or over the phone, and would do so in person when he returned to the rectory at the weekend.

Cat was concerned about them spending so much time together, especially since Kyra had hung up on him on Wednesday, but they seemed to have got over that by Thursday, when Kyra was on the phone to him again.

'Are you going to see Lucas before he goes away this weekend?' Cat asked when Kyra and Francis eventually said goodbye to one another and Kyra joined her and Mary in the sitting room at Amias'.

'Yep. I'm going to meet up with him right now.'

'Doesn't he mind that you're spending so much time with Francis? Either on the phone, in person, or doing research and sharing your findings with him.'

'Nope. I've told him what I'm doing and he told me to knock myself out.'

'Knock yourself out?' Mary queried. 'Why does your boyfriend want you to be unconscious?'

Kyra laughed. 'It's a saying, Gran. It simply means, 'go for it'. He's basically saying that I should spend as much time as I want with Francis.'

'Then why didn't he just say that? Hmm. I wonder if he'd feel the same if he knew you have feelings for Francis?'

'I don't. At least, I don't think I do. I like him a lot but that's all. I've got to dash or I'll be late.'

Cat wasn't sure that what Kyra said about her feelings, was true, but she decided not to press the point and returned to the topic of conversation she and Mary were discussing before Kyra had hurried in to say goodbye.

'Are you sure about the house, Mum?'

'About selling it? Yes I am.'

Mary nodded several times. She'd already said she couldn't bring herself to return to Devon Villa. She had moved into Amias', after two nights with Gladys and Lorna, and had been there ever since. Things were going well, but the situation wasn't without its complications. Mary might now have realised just how wonderful Amias truly was, but it didn't stop her making facetious remarks every so often. Or giving him her advice and opinions when neither were wanted or required. It was as if she simply couldn't help herself. But Amias took it all in his stride and merely smiled, or said he had to be somewhere and dashed off before Mary could make him say something he might regret.

'And the bungalow?'

'I'm going to see it this morning. I was hoping you'd come with me. That's what I was about to ask you before Kyra came in just now. Natalia called, and she's been able to arrange a viewing, although it's not yet officially on the market. Will you come?'

'Of course I will. Right now?'

'In thirty minutes.'

Amias appeared, his phone in his hand.

'It's one of my mates from the police station. They've just got the paperwork. It won't be long before you can return to Devon Villa. Assuming you want to that is. They're sending the letter to you at this address, Mary.'

Mary shivered. 'Thank you. Please thank your friend for letting us know. But I shan't be returning to Devon Villa, other than to move out.'

'Do you want to have a word with him? Do you have any questions?'

Mary shook her head. 'No thank you. Quite frankly, the less I know about this entire episode the happier I shall be.'

Amias smiled sympathetically before glancing at Cat. 'Anything you'd like to ask?'

'No. Not that I can think of.'

They already knew the police weren't continuing with their enquiries after the cellar floor was dug up by the specialists. The body that was found was deemed to be that of Jerusalem Raine, although they were awaiting the results of various tests, including DNA and carbon dating, but along with the confession, it seemed fairly clear it was her. The written confession meant that the coroner was also expected to conclude there was no need for a formal inquest and Jerusalem's body would be released to the Raines and finally laid to rest, although that was unlikely to happen for a week or two at least.

Amias spoke into his phone. 'All good here, thanks. No questions. I'll buy you a pint in the Hope and Anchor tonight if you pop in. I'm meeting Will there. We were supposed to meet up yesterday but one of his clients had an emergency and we had to rearrange. We'll be there from about 7 till 9, if you can make it.' He smiled at Cat again. Blew her a kiss and wandered back the way he'd come.

'Are you OK, Mum?' Cat wrapped an arm around Mary's shoulder.

'Yes. I'm glad that part's over at least.'

'Me too. Now I suppose we can speak to Dennis and see what he can do about the cellar floor. I don't suppose they've left it as they found it.'

'Are you going with Amias tonight?' Mary clearly wanted to change the subject.

'To discuss the VE Day celebrations? No thanks. I was thinking of inviting Abigail over for a glass of wine. And asking you to join us, of course. I have no idea whether Kyra will be here too or if she'll be off again somewhere. I've hardly seen her this week.'

'She's very wrapped up in this Jerusalem and Titus romance.'

'She is. But I'm beginning to wish she'd spend less time on dead people and spend some time sorting out who it is she wants in her life at the moment. Romantically, I mean.'

Chapter Nineteen

The bungalow was better than Cat expected. For some reason she thought it would be dark and dismal and need a total renovation. That was probably because Mary had referred to the owner as 'old Jacob'. But really that should be former owner because Jacob had sadly passed away just a few days ago.

'His daughter put the place on the market before he was even cold,' Gladys said, pouring Cat and Mary cups of coffee. She had seen them arrive, and as they were early, Mary having apparently made a mistake with the time of the appointment, Gladys had invited them in to her home, two doors away.

'I met her once when I was visiting you,' Mary said. 'I didn't like the look of her.'

'Money, money, money.' Gladys rubbed her thumb back and forth across her fingers. 'That's all she was interested in. Mind you, old Jacob wasn't much better. They say he's hidden money all over the place in that bungalow.'

'That'll make a pleasant change. I could do with some extra money and the only things hidden in Devon Villa are worthless paintings, garbled confessions and dead bodies in the cellar.'

Gladys cackled heartily and slapped Mary on the back of her hand and much to Cat's surprise, Mary burst out laughing.

'His wife was here one day and gone the next.' Gladys wiped tears of laughter from the wrinkled skin around her eyes. 'There's a good chance he might have buried her somewhere. But if he did, she's probably in the garden. They hated one another. He didn't want her in the place, alive, so I don't think he'd have kept her there if she was dead.'

Mary and Gladys rocked with amusement.

'How old was Jacob?' Cat asked, more for something to say to stop them laughing so hard. They both looked as if they could have heart attacks at any minute. Even Mary's face was red. Gladys resembled a ripe tomato. One about to burst.

'Old Jacob was seventy-one I believe,' Gladys said, still chuckling.

'Why do you always refer to him as old Jacob then? He wasn't that old, considering. Why not simply, Jacob?'

'Because simply Jacob doesn't make sense.' Gladys looked at her as if she were mad to suggest such a thing.

'No. I meant why not simply use his name? Why not call him Jacob?'

Mary raised her brows. 'Because his name was Bert.' And she and Gladys roared with laughter yet again.

'Bert? Then why do you call him old Jacob?'

'Deary me,' said Gladys. 'Aren't you the one for questions. We call him old Jacob because his name was Bert Morley.'

'And?' Cat didn't understand at all.

'He was a money-grabbing, tight-arsed, grouch. Like Jacob Marley in A Christmas Carol. And he looked just like that actor who played Jacob Marley in the old black and white film. So we called him old Jacob. Not to his face. Or we might all be buried in his garden.'

'What's going on in here?' A cheery voice called out.

'That's my Lorna,' Gladys whispered to Cat, trying to control her cackles. 'You're not flavour of the month as far as she's concerned.'

'Why?'

'Amias Wells.' Gladys tapped her nose.

'Hello, Mary.' Lorna came into the room and smiled. Until she spotted Cat and the smile disappeared. 'Oh. Hello.' Her tone was completely different.

'Hello, Lorna. How are you?'

'Fine, thanks. I didn't know we were

expecting company today, Mum.'

'They've come to see old Jacob's place. Mary might be buying it. Won't that be lovely?'

'Yes. It will.' She didn't look thrilled about it.

'Are you definitely selling Devon Villa then, Mary?'

Mary nodded, having regained her composure. 'I can't live there on my own, especially after this latest nightmare.'

Lorna shot a look at Cat. 'Aren't you and Kyra living there?'

'Yes and no. We're staying at Amias' right now.'

'Of course you are. Excuse me. I need to go and take a shower.' She marched from the room without another word.

'I think that was Natalia Horton's car,' Gladys said, looking at the view through the large picture window, from her comfy chair. 'I saw it from the corner of my eye.'

'We'd better go then,' Mary said, getting to her feet. 'I'll call you later Gladys. Thank you for the coffee. And for the laughter. I really needed that.'

'Always plenty of both here, Mary. You know that. See you again soon, Catherine.'

'We'll show ourselves out,' Mary said. 'You stay there.'

Cat followed Mary to the door but as soon as they were walking down the path, Cat tutted loudly.

'Lorna was bloody rude.'

'She was crazy about Amias, I'm afraid. And she does tend to bear a grudge. Lorna and you will never be friends, I'm sad to say. It would've been nice if you could. But there it is. We can't change that. I'm still certain Natalia said 11.30 but I suppose I could've got it wrong.'

'Hello, you two.' Natalia waved at them before leading them to the front door of the bungalow. 'How are you both? And how is my dear brother? I hardly see him these days. Well not as often as I did. He was always popping in. Not that I'm complaining. I love him to bits but he does drive me mad sometimes. It's so good to see him blissfully happy after all these years. You're a Godsend, Cat. You really are.'

'I hope he thinks that.' Cat beamed at her.

'You know he does.' Natalia winked. 'He may not say it but he loves you more than life.'

'He does say it,' Mary said. 'He tells her every day how much he loves her. I've heard him.'

Cat blushed. 'I hope that's all you've heard.'

'If you're asking if I can hear you having sex, I can't. The walls in that house are thick. I've heard him tell you in the kitchen, and in the sitting room, and on the stairs. He's constantly saying it.'

'Not constantly.' Cat blushed even more

but she was glad the walls were thick in his house. 'He promised me he'd tell me at least once a day, every day for the rest of our lives. And so far, he has.'

'My brother always keeps his promises.' Natalia grinned as she shoved the door open. 'This door may need a bit shaved off the bottom.'

'Don't we all,' said Mary, grinning. 'I'd better not ask Amias. He can't even hammer in a nail.'

'What's this?' Natalia was still grinning.

'Nothing,' Cat said, frowning at Mary. 'Mum's clearly in a rather playful mood right now. Wow. This isn't what I was expecting. I thought old Jacob might've let the place go to wrack and ruin. I mean, Mr. Morley.'

'Don't worry. One or two people in Merriment Bay referred to him as old Jacob. Not just your mum and Gladys and Lorna Carlton. This bungalow is surprising though, isn't it? Follow me and I'll show you around.' She led the way into the kitchen. 'As you can see, it's got a virtually brand-new fitted kitchen with sliding doors straight out to a decked area and one step down to the good-sized garden. There's a new bathroom. The Master bedroom also has an en suite. That's new too. There are two more bedrooms, here and here. There's a heated conservatory leading from the dining room directly out to the garden. A utility room with a door to a paved side garden. He must've spent a fortune having the place done up and that was only a few months before he died. He was supposed to be moving into a home at Easter, so we think he wanted to improve this place to get the best possible price. Not the wisest thing to do in the current market, but great for you, Mary. If you like it that is. You wouldn't have very much to do if you bought the place.'

'Apart from get the front door to open properly. I think it's lovely. What do you think, darling?'

Cat nodded. 'I think it's wonderful. It's closer to us than Devon Villa, and with Gladys and Lorna only two doors away, I'll feel much more at ease.'

'I think I'd like to make an offer.'

'Don't you want to think about it for a little while?' Natalia asked.

'I thought you'd be pleased to make a potential sale.'

'I am, Mary. But I also want you to be sure. You've lived in Devon Villa all your life. It even bears your family name. This isn't going on the market until Monday so you've got at least a couple of days to think about it.'

'I don't need a couple of days, but fine. I'll think about it. And then I'll call you first thing on Monday morning. I'm sorry you won't be getting the sale instructions for Devon Villa, but as I mentioned yesterday, our neighbours' daughter and her family may be potential buyers.'

Natalia nodded and sighed. 'Yes. I'm pleased for all concerned, but I really wanted to sell your house. If they change their minds, or if it falls through, you'll come back to me though, won't you?'

Mary tapped Natalia on the hand. 'You can count on it.'

Chapter Twenty

On that Friday evening, Kyra, Cat, Mary and Amias strolled up Rectory Lane, each carrying either flowers, wine, chocolates, and in Kyra's hands, a Jerusalem artichoke.

'I still think that's in bad taste,' Cat said, glaring at it as if she were hoping she had laser beams in her eyes and could make the vegetable melt away.

'It's a joke, Mum. And Francis will get it, believe me.'

'It's not Francis I'm worried about. It's Constance and Bartholomew.'

'I'll hide it behind my back and give it to him when they're not looking, if that will make you happy.'

'What would make me happy is if you'd leave it out here in the hedges.'

'No can do, Mum.'

'I'd forgotten how twee this place is,' Amias said, grinning at Kyra. 'When those rambling roses grow back later in the year and cover this trellis, and the lavender blooms, this will probably be the perfect country cottage garden.'

'The rectory is hardly a country cottage,' Mary said, giving the faded paintwork of the trellis a look of disgust. 'It has almost as many rooms as Devon Villa. Except the rectory is squat and fat, not unlike Bartholomew, whereas as Devon Villa is tall and elegant.'

'Not unlike you, Gran,' Kyra said, laughing, as they approached the sunshine-yellow front door and rang the Victorian iron bell pull hanging to one side on the white-washed wall.

The door flew open immediately, as if Francis had been waiting just inside to open it.

'Hello.' He beamed at Kyra and then at the others. 'Come in. It's lovely to see you all again.'

'I hope you haven't invited us all here to tell us more unpleasant news about poor Jerusalem,' Mary said. 'What with the police, the coroner, the local and even the regional media attention, that all began today, I really wish we'd never discovered that cellar. Let's hope the national press don't get wind of it.'

'I can only imagine how difficult it's been having journalists running around asking questions and trying to dig up dirt. They've been here too. And to Wynter House, I believe. But that's not because of Jerusalem, of course.' He glanced at Cat and coughed. 'Let me take your coats. I see you're wearing one this evening, Kyra.'

'It hasn't been easy,' Cat said, as Kyra stuck out her tongue at Francis. 'It all blew up this morning. But we've all asked for them to respect our privacy. Both regarding Jerusalem and also my new-found family. We're hoping they'll just write what they'll write and go away. It's not really anyone else's business, is it? Rafe's given them a brief statement and also asked for privacy. I really don't understand why any of it is of interest to the general public. The Wynters aren't aristocracy. Or famous. Although the Wyntersleap Gin is getting a lot of good reviews. We Devons are certainly not famous. I'm fairly well-known in certain circles for my paintings, but again, of no real interest to the mainstream. But I suppose nothing much ever happens in Merriment Bay so any story is better than none.'

Kyra smiled. 'But Rafe did say that visitor ticket sales for the Wynter House tours have shot through the roof in just a matter of hours, and that there's also been a phenomenal amount of new interest in the Wyntersleap Gin Tours. So I suppose it's had an upside. And that's all in one day. We don't know if it's because of the long-lost sibling bit, or because the long-lost sibling also appears to be descended from a thief and a murderer.'

'Kyra!' Cat glared at her.

'What? I'm simply stating the truth.'

'Good evening.' Constance and Bartholomew appeared in the hall. 'Do come through to the sitting room. There's a lovely fire in the hearth. It's turned very cold again.'

Kyra hung back, slowly taking off her coat with one hand.

'What's the matter with your other hand?' Francis asked, hanging everyone else's coats and scarves on the rack. 'Do you need some help?'

'Nope. Ta dah!'

She produced the artichoke from behind her back and he looked at it for a moment or two before a grin swept across his face.

'For me? You shouldn't have. I've always wanted my very own artichoke. Oh! Is this a symbol of you giving me your heart? I'll treasure it forever.'

Kyra frowned, and gave him a playful slap. 'No, you idiot. It's a Jerusalem artichoke. Jerusalem. Get it? The heart comes from a globe artichoke, not a Jerusalem.'

The grin turned into a laugh. 'Of course I got it. I'm teasing you. But look at it.' He twisted the large tuber around. 'It's sort of heart-shaped, don't you think?'

It was, from the angle at which he was holding it, but she hadn't noticed that when she bought it at the Merriment Bay market that morning. The long, large tuber did resemble a thin, elongated heart.

'Nope. I hope Constance has cooked dinner because I'm starving, and I don't suppose you can boil an egg.'

'That's rather judgemental. And also somewhat sexist. I'll have you know I'm pretty handy in the kitchen.' He moved closer. 'I'm pretty handy in other rooms too.'

She shoved him aside, tutting loudly. 'But sadly, you're pretty crap at chat up lines. And I've got a boyfriend, remember?'

'Sadly, I do. And you look stunning again tonight. You're more conservatively dressed this time. Is this to show solidarity with me?' He was grinning broadly.

'You're an idiot. It's because both Mum and Gran lectured me for about an hour about what I'd planned to wear. "You can't wear that to a rectory" was just one of the many comments. I had to wear this boring, knee-length dress or I wouldn't have been allowed to come.'

'What were you planning on wearing then? I'm dying to know.'

'Die away, because I'm not saying.'

'Fine. It's a very pretty dress. Come on. Let's join the others. I'll leave this here for now in case I get asked questions.'

He put the vegetable on a small table and nodded his head towards the door of what was obviously the sitting room.

Kyra saw everyone was seated by the time she walked in. The only vacant seats were on the sofa. A two-seater sofa. Meaning she would have no choice but to sit beside Francis, and closer than she would've liked. Speaking to him on the phone this week had sent tingles racing through her. Seeing him again and breathing in the mild scent of his aftershave was giving her goosebumps up and down her arms. Sitting next to him on the sofa might give her more than goosebumps.

Bartholomew was pouring everyone drinks, and he proudly held up a bottle of Wyntersleap Gin.

'A wonderful gift from Rafe. He's such a generous man. And so calm and pleasant even in the face of all this gossip. I want you to know, Catherine, Kyra and Mary, that Constance and I won't be a party to any of it. We were surprised, of course, as was everyone in Merriment Bay. We all thought Alwick was the … well, that doesn't matter. It's none of anyone's busy but yours, and dear Rafe and Adam. Oh, and Olivia too. I called there today to see how that dear sweet lady is, after her heart attack, but unfortunately she was too unwell to receive visitors. Even me.'

'Yes, Uncle,' Francis said, clearly trying to change the subject. 'But that's not why we've invited you all here this evening.'

'Why have you invited us?' Mary said. 'I

181

assume it's not merely for dinner.'

She was glaring at Bartholomew as if she'd like to step on him and grind him into the ground at that precise moment in time. Even though he was the vicar. Kyra smiled at that image. The vicar did look a bit like a beetle this evening with his black trousers, black waistcoat and black cardigan buttoned down the front over a white shirt and his big round belly.

Francis shook his head. 'To tell you what I've discovered. But it does concern Jerusalem, so perhaps I'll tell you now and then we can talk of other things for the rest of the evening. I've been researching the records and I don't think that confession was written by George Devon, as we all assumed.'

'Why not?' Amias asked. 'Are you suggesting it's a forgery?'

'No. No it's definitely not a forgery. Something bothered me about it at the time but I wasn't sure what. I took a photo of it on my phone and I've been going over and over it and finally realised what it was. Well, two things actually. The first is the wording. It's all a bit flowery for a man. The second is the handwriting. That's definitely on the feminine side, I think.'

'Now who is being sexist?' Kyra smiled at him sarcastically.

'Point taken. But it's true. My research came up with the answer. George wasn't the only person living in Devon Villa at the time. His wife was dead, but he had a son and a daughter. The son was away at sea all that year. The year of 1826. Like Jerusalem's husband, Edward Raine, George's son, who was also called George. George Thomas Henry Devon, was in the navy.'

'You're looking a bit confused, Gran.' Kyra interrupted Francis again.

'Not confused, darling. Merely wondering when Francis will get to the point.'

Kyra grinned and so did Francis.

'I'm getting there. It's the daughter who concerns us. A daughter who was twenty-nine and unmarried. Her name was Georgiana Elizabeth Mary Devon. I think she was the one who killed Jerusalem. And I think she did it in "a fit of madness", as the confession states, her "heart being consumed with a jealous rage, hitherto unbeknownst to me". At least I think it says "a jealous rage". I can't quite make that bit out. But it does make sense. According to the Coroner's Office, Jerusalem was stabbed. Probably more than once. I know someone who works there so he told me the findings, before the report is filed. They know that because of marks on her ribs.'

'That could happen in a jealous rage, I suppose,' Kyra said. 'But why steal the painting? And how did Jerusalem get into the cellar?'

'I'm not sure the painting was stolen. I've been thinking about what you said about Jerusalem possibly wanting to sell it. I don't think she did. I'm sure it meant too much to her. But what if her husband, Edward was coming home? Possibly earlier than expected? They were often at sea for months, or even years, in those days, so she would've been safe with the painting being on display until he returned. But he would recognise the woman in the painting was his wife and the man wasn't him. I know from her journals that Edward had blond hair. And from the records of the trial everyone says the painting had been hanging on the wall in Jerusalem's bedroom when it was stolen. What if she wanted to hide the painting until he returned to sea? She couldn't hide it in the rectory in case he found it. Don't forget, the rectory then was only half the size of this one. This was built in 1858, more than twenty years after Jerusalem's death. What if she and Georgiana were friends? Or she thought they were.'

'Wait,' Cat said. 'You think Jerusalem carried that painting to the house that stood where Devon Villa now stands, and asked her *friend* to keep it safely hidden, and Georgiana took her to the cellar and they locked the painting in the coffer and then Georgiana was overwhelmed with jealousy and stabbed her friend to death?'

Francis shrugged. 'It's a hypothesis. Georgiana was a spinster. At twenty-nine, in those days, she probably believed there wasn't much chance of her ever being married. Jerusalem had a husband, a son, and a rather fit and handsome lover, if the painting and the descriptions of Titus are anything to go by.'

Amias grinned. 'He was a Wells. Of course he was fit and handsome. But would this woman really stab her friend because of that?'

'It's been done before,' Mary said. 'And some women do fight over men. That's not so hard to believe. Lorna Carlton was rather rude to Catherine simply because you love my daughter and not her.'

'What? When did this happen?' Amias demanded.

Cat tutted. 'It was nothing. She simply left the room, that's all. We were in her home so she had every right to ignore me if she wanted to. Not that she did ignore me. She said hello. I don't know why Mum mentioned it and I don't want to hear another word about it. Let's concentrate on Jerusalem.'

Amias took Cat's hand in his as if he wanted to protect her.

'I'm sorry,' Mary said.

Cat nodded at her. 'I have a slight issue with why the coffer was in the cellar, rather than in a room in the house, Francis. You said it was Jacobean and good quality.'

'Ooh!' Kyra said. 'Perhaps it was in Georgiana's room and that's where she stabbed Jerusalem. With a letter opener, maybe.'

'Not in the library with a candlestick?' Cat said, grinning.

Kyra tutted and continued: 'Jerusalem fell on the coffer and died and Georgiana couldn't bear to look at it again when she realised what she'd done. She told her dad, who buried the body in the cellar and put the coffer with the painting still inside on top.'

'But why bury her in the cellar?' Amias queried. 'Why not dispose of her body somewhere else?'

'Maybe they planned to, but something went wrong,' Kyra said, almost picturing the entire thing from start to finish. 'Perhaps they were scared of being seen. The servants might've had a night off, or something, so George dragged the coffer to the cellar and carried Jerusalem's body down. Then maybe he decided the cellar was the perfect place to bury her. No one would find the body as long as he and his daughter lived in the house. He might've told the son when George junior got back from sea.'

'I think I know why they chose the cellar,' Francis said. 'The servants did all have that night off. And not just the night. They had the entire day off that day because it was the day of the Midsummer Fayre in Merriment Bay. I've been checking, but I do remember reading about that on a previous occasion. The streets would've been packed with revellers. George couldn't risk being seen transporting and disposing of a body and he couldn't keep it hidden in the house. So he, possibly with Georgiana's assistance, or with the help of a friend – but obviously *not* Obadiah Raine, decided to take the opportunity of not having servants around and to bury the body in the cellar. It would've taken one or two people a couple of hours to dig up that floor. It wasn't as solid as I thought it would be, apparently. Yes. I also talked to the specialists who dug it up. I like to know all the facts. Anyway, George could've then dragged the coffer downstairs and put that on top to hide the fact the floor had been disturbed. Oh, and I've discovered something else. I've found the plans of the house that stood there at the time. It was Tudor, as we thought it might be, and quite a grand affair, and interestingly, the door to the cellar was actually in the hall. The servants might not have been allowed access to it at all. The Devons might've kept it locked. I don't know if that's true, but it would explain things.'

'And because Jerusalem was stabbed, they couldn't say her death was an accident.' Kyra shook her head.

'Exactly.' Francis nodded.

Cat tutted. 'So they decided to frame Titus

Wells instead. I'm disgusted with my ancestors. If Jerusalem and Georgiana were friends, Jerusalem might have told her how she felt about Titus and how Titus felt about her. Another reason why Georgiana was so jealous. She and her dad would probably have panicked, and she might have told him about Titus and they made the story up about him stealing the painting and murdering Jerusalem, because they were panicking. They might have thought he would get off due to lack of evidence. Unless they were completely evil people. And I'd like to think they weren't. Not entirely. I'd like to believe they felt at least a pang of guilt.'

'Perhaps that's why the chairs were there,' Constance said, and all eyes turned to her.

'Er. Why?' Kyra asked.

'Because Georgiana and her father would sit down there and pray for both the Good Lord's and Jerusalem's forgiveness.'

'I certainly wouldn't sit in a cellar with a dead body,' Mary said. 'They could go to the church to pray for that.'

'Nor would I,' said Kyra. 'But I can see what Constance means. People were very religious in those days. If they were guilt-ridden, perhaps they thought it might help. And knowing her body was right there, made them think they were closer to her.'

'And she might hear them?' Francis teased.

'If they were guilt-ridden they should've confessed,' Amias said. 'They shouldn't have let Titus hang for a crime he didn't commit.'

'We'll never know the truth,' Francis said, with an air of disappointment. 'I think Georgiana left that confession hidden in that secret drawer, hoping that one day, someone would find it and set the record straight. She knew her father would never let her confess and ruin the Devon name. He'd probably have had her locked away in a sanitorium if she'd tried. They weren't pleasant places to be. But I know he didn't do that because she lived in the house until the day she died, unmarried, at the age of forty-five.'

'What about her father?' Kyra asked.

'Her father outlived both her and her brother, who died at sea. I think it was possibly after her death that he boarded up the cellar. He married again when he was sixty-eight, and had another son before he died in his early seventies. This one was called Henry George Horatio Devon. Henry and his own son were the ones who rebuilt the house in various stages. Whether they knew about the contents of the cellar, or even that it was there, is anyone's guess. Although they must've had the foundations strengthened, I wouldn't thought, and if they did, I'm sure they would've found the coffer. But again, that's something we'll never know. At least Jerusalem will finally rest

189

in peace.'

Amias nodded. 'And Titus will have his name cleared, at least in Merriment Bay.'

Cat grinned suddenly. 'I'm not sure you should tell your dad about Francis' research. He's always said the Devon women bring nothing but trouble.'

Amias looked her in the eye. 'That's true. He always did say that. But now that we're together, he seems willing to accept that's not necessarily true. And I can't lie, Cat.'

'I know you can't. I wouldn't want you to. And the fact is, he's right. A Devon woman killed Jerusalem and either framed Titus or at the very least, let him pay for crimes he didn't commit. We'll have to accept that, whether we like it or not. I just hope Alwick won't blame us for it.'

'I don't think he will. Not now. And even if he does, now that he's in love, he's definitely mellowed.'

'Love does that,' Constance said. 'Love changes people and brings out the best in them.'

'Not always,' Mary said. 'But it does change people. I will agree with you on that.'

Kyra glanced at Francis and saw he was looking at her.

'I'm starving,' she said, quickly looking away. 'And something smells delicious.'

Chapter Twenty-One

Mary thought about the bungalow all weekend. She discussed it on the phone with Gladys and with Annie. She wrote a list of pros and cons both of Devon Villa and of the bungalow, but that didn't really help.

'Devon Villa has so many pros,' she said, when she, Cat and Amias sat down to dinner on the Sunday evening. 'The bungalow only has a few. It's smaller. It's easier and cheaper to maintain. It's closer to this house, and very close to Gladys. It may have money hidden somewhere.'

'Seriously, Gran?' Kyra asked.

'Have you really added that to the list?' Cat gave her a mockingly look.

'Only as a joke. The list of pros is short. I'll miss so much about Devon Villa. The list of pros for that is long. Very long. But it does have one or two cons. And they're big ones. I miss Mother when I'm there. I miss her here, but it doesn't seem quite so painful here. Devon Villa now reminds me of Jeremy, and of being taken for a fool. Again, that doesn't feel so bad when I'm here, or at Gladys'. And, of course, the big one. There was a body in the cellar. No matter what, I don't want to live there knowing that one of our ancestors murdered a friend and buried her like that. We Devon women are strong. But this has made me realise that perhaps, that isn't always such a good thing to be. There are some things that one simply can't live with, and a body having been buried in my cellar, for me, is one of them.'

She tore up the list and sighed. 'I want to call Natalia first thing in the morning and make an offer on the bungalow. And I want to speak to Dennis Grey and see if his daughter and her family are genuinely interested in buying Devon Villa. But there is one thing I want to request. I want the name of the house to remain. Don't ask me why, but that's feels very important to me.'

'I can't see that being a problem,' Cat said. 'Isn't it unlucky to change the name of a house, in any event? Or is that boats?'

Amias grinned. 'No idea. Let's speak to Natalia and get things moving, but only if you're certain, Mary. There's no rush for you to move from here. You can sell the house and stay here until you find something else that you prefer, if you've got doubts about the bungalow.'

'That's kind. But I do like the bungalow. Although I will miss the view of the sea.'

'Then wait, Mum. Until we can find you somewhere with a view of the sea.'

'That's rarer than bodies in cellars, I should think. At least in Merriment Bay. I will ask Natalia though. Just in case. But in the meantime, I want to get things moving. I'll need you all to help me decide what to keep from Devon Villa, as far as the furniture and everything is concerned. And that includes you, Amias. I think of you as a part of this family now.'

Chapter Twenty-Two

Cat and Kyra had something else to keep them occupied during all the various dramas going on around them. They had agreed to paint the trompe l'oeil Neva wanted on one of the walls of The Mane Event. Neither of them had ever done anything like it, and they had never worked on a piece of art together, but they were both artists and Cat was sure it would be fun to do, and possibly add another string to their respective bows.

Neva and her friend and business partner, Jo both wanted it to be of the Roman goddess, Venus rising from the waves in her seashell, her long locks flowing as if caught in a summer's breeze, and Cat and Kyra used images of Botticelli's famous painting to guide them. The colours were to be light and bright, depicting summer, yet at the same time, not too 'in your face'. Neva wanted the painting to exude peace and tranquillity, and for the colours to reflect that. Soft blues for the sky, cerulean blues for the sea, the gentle waves edged with pearl white, buttercup and cornflower yellows for the sun and for Venus' hair, pale honey for the sand, a shimmering pearlescent ivory for the shell and dove grey and cream for the seagulls that Neva decided she wanted added.

Cat and Kyra did a rough sketch on paper, followed by another rough outline on the wall, before tackling the final painting. They worked well together and they worked every day for four hours in the mornings for almost a week. Neva and Jo worked around them, finishing the other walls, moving furniture, adding touches here and there until Cat and Kyra made their final brushstrokes and the artwork was complete.

Cat and Kyra were pleased with it, and thankfully, Neva and Jo were delighted.

'I love it,' Neva said. 'How much do I owe you? I'll pay you right away.'

They hadn't actually agreed a price beforehand. Cat wasn't sure how it would turn out, despite her years of experience and the fact that she was a talented artist whose work could command fairly high prices in several galleries across the UK. Her paintings had even sold to overseas buyers. But a trompe l'oeil on a wall in a hairdressing salon was a new experience for her and one that, oddly enough, she had been nervous about.

Neva had effectively said that whatever it cost would be fine by her. She and Jo had the sales proceeds from their flat in London and it seemed they weren't working to a budget. Cat did suggest they might like to think about setting one, but they both smiled and said this business was their dream come true and they wanted the salon to be perfect.

'It won't cost more than a few hundred pounds,' Cat had said. 'You're dating my brother so we'll give you a massive discount.'

'In that case,' Neva had replied. 'We'll throw in a few months-worth of haircuts, blow drys and beauty treatments.'

On the day Cat and Kyra lay down their brushes, they both agreed they wouldn't charge Neva and Jo a penny.

'We don't want you to pay us,' Cat said. 'This has been such a pleasure for both of us and we're giving it to you and Jo as your moving in cum opening gift. Although we will take you up on the offer of a few haircuts and beauty treatments.'

Neva and Jo were overjoyed and actually rather emotional. They hugged and kissed Cat and Kyra, shedding one or two tears of joy in the process.

'This calls for champagne,' Jo said, dashing out to The Merry Shopper to buy some and returning fifteen minutes or so later with cakes as well as three bottles of bubbly.

'It's the Merriment Bay Moonlight Valentine's Dance on Friday,' Neva said, as the four of them sat, squeezed together on the large, multi-coloured sofa that had been left by the previous owner. They were all admiring the trompe l'oeil and had already raised several glasses to Venus, to Botticelli, to dreams and new beginnings, to life and love, to family and friends, and finally to themselves and their new-found friendship. 'I can't do anything on the actual day, 'cos Rafe and I are doing something special. No idea what, 'cos he hasn't told me. He wants it to be a surprise.' She gave a little hiccough and was clearly trying not to slur her words. 'But I can do something on Thursday. That's the day before. Tomorrow, in fact. For you and for Kyra and also for your mum, if you like. It'll be a dry run for us to see whether everything in the salon works as it should before we open for business. I want everything to be perfect.'

'Talking of dry runs,' Jo said. 'My glass is empty.'

'Are you sure?' Cat asked.

'Yes,' Jo said, holding her glass upside down. 'See. Empty.'

Cat laughed in a drunken fashion and nudged Jo's arm. 'No. Silly. I meant about the haircuts and stuff.'

Neva nodded repeatedly as she passed Jo the bottle and Jo topped up her glass.

'Yep,' Neva said.

'Yep,' Jo agreed, taking a large gulp of champagne and sighing loudly. 'I needed that. I was as parched as a pearl on a pebble patio. Here's to you, Venus. And to love.'

'To Venus and to love.' They all raised their glasses.

Jo slumped deeper into the back cushion. 'I think I'm in love with Gavin, you know. Well, in lust, at least.'

'Gavin?' Cat queried.

'The gorgeous hunk who works at Wynter House. He's the groundsman, or gardener, or whatever.'

'Oh yes. Rafe introduced us,' Cat said. 'He is handsome. Is he single?'

'Completely. The problem is he doesn't seem in a hurry not to be. Single, I mean. He avoided me for ages when I first met him but we're friends now. Just friends. No matter how much I flirt or how obvious I make it that I'm interested, he doesn't take the hint.'

'Perhaps he's gay,' said Kyra.

'Nope. Definitely not gay. Just not interested in me.'

'He's mad,' Neva said. 'I keep asking Rafe to ask him if he likes her but Rafe grins and says he's not getting involved in Gavin's love life and that if Gavin does like her, he'll tell her himself in his own good time.'

'You might have a long wait,' Cat said. 'It

took Amias more than eighteen years to tell me he'd loved me all his life. Well, not all his life. But ever since I met him.'

'To be fair, Mum. It also took you the same amount of time to tell him how you felt about him. Did that just make sense?'

'Totally,' Jo said. 'I don't want to wait eighteen years. I haven't had sex since before Christmas.'

'You could ask him out,' Kyra said.

'You could ask him to marry you,' Neva added. 'It's a leap year. Women can propose to men on leap years.'

Kyra tutted. 'Women can propose to men on any day of any year. But not many do. So much for equality. Why is that? Why do most women wait to be asked?'

'Because it's romantic,' Neva said. 'I'd rather be asked than ask. But Kyra's right, Jo. You could ask Gavin out.'

'True. I could. But if he said no it would be *sooooo* embarrassing.'

'I asked Amias.' Cat tried to sit upright but failed. 'I asked him how he felt about me. It was on New Year's Eve and we've been together ever since. He took me home to his beautiful house and we made wonderful love all night and again in the morning and every day afterwards.'

'Thanks Mum. Too much information.'

'Rafe is so good in bed,' Neva said. 'I wasn't

sure he would be but he is. I really, really love him.'

'I really love Amias.' Cat grinned at Neva.

'I love Gavin, I think. I'm sure he'd be good in bed. Here's to me finding out one day very, very soon.' Jo clinked her glass with everyone's and then she looked at Kyra and gave her a poke with her fingers.

'And what about you, Kyra? Who're you in love with?'

Kyra looked thoughtful and slowly shook her head. 'I wish I knew.' She emptied her glass and held it out for a refill.

'Lucas!' Cat said. 'You love Lucas Lester. Don't you, sweetheart?'

Kyra sighed. 'I don't know, Mum. I thought I did, but now I'm not so sure.'

'Ooooh,' said Jo, snuggling closer. 'Is there someone else? Or does he just get on your nerves now? I thought I loved my fiancé. Turns out I didn't. He got on my nerves. But not as much as Charmaine. She's his mum. So anyway, Kyra. Tell us all about it.'

'Sadly there's nothing much to tell. I'm dating Lucas. I do love him, I think. But I also think I might be falling for someone else.'

'Francis Raine?' Cat asked, even though she already knew the answer.

'Francis Raine.' Kyra nodded.

'Francis Raine,' repeated Neva and Jo in unison.

'I like that more than Lucas Lester,' Jo said.

'Me too,' said Neva. 'But it's not about a name, is it? It's about how you feel in here.' She pointed her finger at her heart.

'That's the problem,' Kyra said. 'I'm not sure how I feel.'

'Well, here's to Francis Raine.' Jo held her glass in the air.

'To Francis Raine.' Neva did the same.

'To sorting myself out,' Kyra said, holding up her glass. 'And sooner rather than later.'

'I'll definitely drink to that,' Cat said.

Chapter Twenty-Three

On Thursday morning, Cat and Kyra spent several hours sleeping off the champagne.

Amias made them coffee, followed by breakfast, followed by more coffee, none of which either of them touched.

'I've got to go to work,' Amias said, kissing Cat on the cheek. 'I've got a couple of lessons at the reservoir. Will you be OK?'

Cat grunted in reply.

'Nod for yes.'

Cat grunted again and moved her head just a fraction.

'OK. I love you. I'll see you later. Oh. And it's almost 11.30, in case you need to get up. Didn't you say you were going to Neva's salon just after lunch?'

Cat grunted for a third time.

'I've put some painkillers and a glass of water on your bedside table.'

A knock on the open, bedroom door made

Cat wince. Mary's voice made her try to hide her head beneath the pillow.

'Catherine! For goodness sake. Why are you still in bed? Get up, darling. You need to shower, dress and get some air. You'll be spending several hours in a chair at Neva's salon this afternoon.'

'I've tried,' Amias said. 'I think she needs more sleep. I've got to go.'

'Yes, yes,' Mary said. 'Leave her to me.'

'I'm not sure I like the sound of that.' He gave a little laugh.

'I'm not sure Catherine will either. But that's the price one must pay for imbibing copious amounts of alcohol. She'll be fine. I promise.'

Cat heard Amias say goodbye once more and she settled down into the pillow, only to be rudely awakened by a wet flannel in her face and the duvet being swept back to expose her naked body.

'Mum!' she shrieked, tugging at the duvet.

'Get up, darling. I'm not leaving this room until you're in that shower.'

'Good morning!' Natalia's cheerful voice boomed out from the hall and she marched into the bedroom.

Cat hurriedly covered herself, blushing profusely. It was bad enough that her mum had seen her naked. But what on earth was Natalia doing in the bedroom?

'Good morning, Natalia,' Mary said. 'You look lovely today. Which is more than can be said for my darling daughter.'

'Thank you, Mary. So do you. Is Cat in a bad way? She did sound really pissed. I mean drunk, yesterday evening.'

'She hasn't eaten a thing. She hasn't even touched her coffee.'

'Yes. That's what Amias said.'

'Amias?' Cat mumbled. 'Where is he?'

'Gone to give someone lessons at the reservoir,' Natalia said. 'I arrived just as he was leaving.'

'Oh yes. I remember he said that.'

Cat forced herself up onto one elbow and reached out for the water and the painkillers, swallowing them back as fast as she could.

'Right then,' Natalia said. 'Shall I make brunch? We've got a busy day ahead and you need to have some food inside you.'

'Er. Busy day? Did we have something planned? I hope I haven't screwed things up, Nat. Mum, Kyra and I are supposed to be going to Neva's salon for a bit of pampering.'

'I know. I'm joining you. Neva invited me last night.'

'She did? That's nice.'

'Yeah. It was when you called for advice.' A huge grin spread across Natalia's face. 'You don't remember calling me, do you?'

Cat frowned. 'Last night? No. Sorry. To be

honest I don't remember very much at all about last night. I don't even remember getting into bed.' She rubbed her hand across her forehead.

'Amias put you to bed,' Mary said, shaking her head.

'Oh. Was he cross?'

Natalia burst out laughing. 'He wouldn't be cross about that. So you don't remember calling me, but does that mean you weren't serious?'

'Serious? About what?'

'About asking Amias to marry you. That's what you told me you were going to do. And you said you wanted my advice because if you left it up to him, he'd never get around to asking you. Which is true. He won't. Not because he doesn't want to. He wants to marry you more than he wants anything in this world, I'm positive about that. It's really odd. He's strong, he's clever, he's courageous, and he doesn't give a damn what people think of him. But when it comes to you, my darling brother turns into a lump of quivering jelly and has no idea what to say or do.'

Cat smiled. That wasn't entirely true. On New Year's Eve, once they had finally kissed, he'd known precisely what to say and do, and he'd said and done it ever since. But would he summon up the courage to ask her to marry him one day? He'd told her that first night that he'd wanted to scream from the rooftops that he loved her. He'd wanted to take her in his arms and tell her. He'd wanted to march into her house and declare his feelings. But every time he got close to thinking he could do it, sheer terror always engulfed him. He had loved her for so long that he was terrified of losing her for good. At least if he didn't tell her how he felt she couldn't tell him to get lost. It was completely irrational, possibly even a little crazy, but that was how he felt. Until that wonderful moment when she had told him she loved him.

'You're planning to propose to Amias?' Mary sounded incredulous.

'Apparently I am. I can't remember saying so, or phoning Nat to ask for advice. But I love him, Mum. No. I adore him. And yes. I want to marry him.'

'I'm glad to hear it. But women don't propose to men, Catherine. They wait to be asked. Although I do see that with Amias, that may pose a problem.'

'But why do we wait? Even Kyra questioned that last night, I seem to recall.'

'You told me on the phone that you were going to do it because this year is a leap year and you're going to take the bull by the horns. I'm not sure if you meant Amias was the bull, or the marriage proposal was, but anyway. You wanted me to help you decide how to do it. So here I am. Ready, waiting and eager to get started. You, it seems, not so much.'

Chapter Twenty-Four

The Merriment Bay Moonlight Valentine's Dance was being held in the main assembly hall of St Mary's School opposite the church, as it was every year and had been since Constance Raine and other members of the Merriment Bay W.I. had organised the first dance more than twenty years ago.

Cat could still remember the only one she had attended. She was with Kyle but she had spent quite a lot of time trying to stop her gaze from wandering to Amias and the girl he'd brought with him.

She couldn't recall who the girl was now, and Amias had probably forgotten his date within a week or two of the dance. He never seemed to stay with anyone for more than a few weeks in those days.

At the time she'd thought he was merely living up to his 'bad boy' reputation, but now she knew it was because he was in love with her. And no other girl, or woman, had ever been able to capture his heart. Or keep his interest.

It made her feel like a million dollars. But it also made her feel sad. They had wasted so many years. And in Amias' case, broken several hearts along the way. But they were together now and that's all that mattered.

Sometimes though, she would wake up in the night and look at him. The gorgeous, virile man sleeping beside her. And she couldn't help but wonder, just for a second or two in those early hours when everyone's biggest fears stalk them and circle their beds, whether now that he had got her, he might wonder what all the fuss was about. Whether he might lose interest in her. And whether she really had captured his heart forever.

Then he would open his eyes as if he could feel, even in his sleep, that she was looking at him, and his eyes would fill with love and wonder and passion. A smile would creep onto his lips, growing broader by the second, and he would reach out and touch her.

'I love you,' he'd whisper, somehow knowing she longed to hear that, despite the fact he said it every single day. Usually several times.

'I love you too,' she'd reply.

Then he'd pull her close and kiss her. Often, they'd make love. Sleepy, tender love, but sometimes they would both close their eyes and go back to sleep, Cat reassured yet again that Amias truly loved her with all his heart and every fibre of his being, and that she felt the same about him.

Their love would last forever. She was certain of that.

She was also certain that she wanted to be Mrs Catherine Wells more than anything in the world.

And what better time to ask him to marry her than at the Merriment Bay Moonlight Valentine's Dance?

At least that's what Natalia, Mary, Neva and Jo all agreed. Cat wasn't one hundred per cent sure that Valentine's Day actually was the best time, and Kyra also seemed uncertain.

Cat asked her again as they were getting ready. She popped into Kyra's room and stretched out across the bed.

'Am I making a mistake, sweetheart?'

'About asking Amias to marry you? Absolutely not. You adore one another.'

'I know. I meant about asking him tonight. At the Merriment Bay Moonlight Valentine's Dance.' She couldn't help but smile every time she said that.

'The Merriment Bay Moonlight Valentine's Dance.' Kyra laughed. 'Only Constance could come up with a name like that.' She shook her head and sighed. 'It's romantic, Mum. Of course it is. To get the dance floor cleared of people and stand in the middle of the hall. Just you and Amias. And to ask him to marry you in front of everyone in Merriment Bay. But it's also a bit of a cliché, don't you think? And I know Jo loved the idea of the heart-shaped balloons falling down around you once he's said yes. And of the band playing your favourite song. But I'm not entirely on board with the whole thing. And I know he won't, but can you imagine if he said no? How awful would that be?'

Cat sat bolt upright. 'Do you think he might? Oh dear God, Kyra. What if he does?' Her heart pounded against her chest; a cold sweat broke out across her brow, her breath came in short, sharp gasps.

'No!' Kyra dashed to the bed, sat down and wrapped her arms around Cat. 'I don't know why I said that. He'll definitely say yes. Not even the tiniest shred of a doubt about that. I was just picturing the whole thing and that suddenly popped into my head. Forget I said it. That will never happen. He'll say yes before you've finished the little speech you've written.'

Cat took several deep breaths until she was able to speak again. 'And now I'm not sure about that either. Oh dear God, Kyra. I don't think I can do this.'

'Then don't. Not tonight. Wait until another night.'

'But it's all been arranged. Taryn Small will sing, 'Be My Lucky Valentine' then she'll ask everyone to clear the floor but I'll pretend my heel is caught and I'll hold on to Amias until it's just him and me left standing there. Then I'll do my speech. And, if he says yes. Oh God he must say yes. He will. I'm sure he will. So he'll say yes and then the balloons will come down and Taryn will sing 'Maybe This Time' by Michael Murphy. Not the other one she thought I meant. And we'll dance and then everyone will join us and ... and...'

'Wish you both well and congratulate you. Yes, Mum. That's the plan. But Neva can tell Taryn the plan has changed. She needn't clear the hall. She can sing another song. Or she can still sing that one and you and Amias can just dance to it. The balloons can still come down over everyone dancing. That'll be fun. And Amias will never know there had been a plan. Is that what you'd rather do?'

Cat looked her in the eye. 'I don't know, sweetheart. I honestly don't know. But I do want to be his wife. I want that so much it actually hurts to think about it.'

'You can be. Just ask him another time.'

'May I come in?' Mary called through the closed door.

'Yes,' Kyra shouted.

'Oh. You're both here.' She gave an awkward smile.

'What's wrong, Mum? You're looking anxious.'

'Anxious isn't it, exactly.' Mary gave Kyra an odd look. 'It's just that I've been thinking about this proposal and I wanted to have a word with Kyra about it.'

'Why?' Cat met her eye. 'If you've got anything to say about it you should say it to me. I'm the one doing the proposing.'

'Precisely. And I just don't like it. I've never been one for such public displays, as you know. Proposals should be romantic. They should be a man asking the woman he loves to be his wife. If you feel you have to do the asking, then fine. I'll reluctantly go along with that. But not at the Merriment Bay Moonlight Valentine's Dance, darling. I mean, what if the man says no? You'd be completely humiliated.'

'Yes. Thank you, Mum. Kyra's already given me a panic attack about that. Are you saying you don't think I should go ahead with the plan for tonight because you think Amias might say no? Or are you saying you don't like the plan at all?'

'I'm almost certain he'll say yes. But I still don't like the plan.'

Cat let out a sigh. 'We've just been discussing the same thing. I'm not sure I want to go through with it. I'm still going to ask him to marry me though. Just not tonight. It does feel a bit tacky, somehow.'

'It's also rather selfish,' Mary said. 'People have paid to be at this dance to do precisely that. To dance and have fun. Not to watch you ask Amias Wells to make an honest woman of you.'

Cat and Kyra exchanged glances and Kyra burst out laughing.

'Oh, Gran. Sometimes you're just so old-fashioned. Anyone would think you're in your late nineties, not your early sixties.'

'With everything that's been going on since you and your mother came home to Merriment Bay, I feel as if I am in my late nineties. But are you saying the proposal is off? Are you going to tell Natalia?'

'Yes. I'll call her now. And Neva too. She'll hopefully speak to Taryn before I do. I'll go and get my phone.' Cat stood up and ambled towards the door. 'It's odd though. I was really looking forward to being an engaged woman by the end of tonight.'

Chapter Twenty-Five

The Merriment Bay Moonlight Valentine's Dance was a huge success. The hall was festooned with heart-shaped bunting. The heart-shaped, red balloons dropped from the sky as planned only not to Cat and Amias' song; to the song 'Ninety-nine Red Balloons', instead. Food and drink sales soared, all the proceeds going to local charities as always. Everyone danced until the early hours, and made their way home in the pouring rain. Not quite the weather people had hoped for. But 14th February in Merriment Bay was never going to be a balmy night.

Kyra and Cat danced with several people, not just with Lucas and Amias. Rafe and Adam asked them to dance, as did Gavin, the man who Jo Duncan was in love with. Or at least in lust with. Gavin did dance with Jo once or twice, that Kyra saw, but he seemed to be spending much of his time talking and dancing with Judith, who was Rafe and Olivia's assistant. Kyra and Cat had met her when they went to Wynter House for Sunday lunch.

'Gavin and Judith seem very friendly,' Kyra said to Cat and Amias, and Neva and Rafe overheard as they were standing right beside them.

'They've been friends for years,' Rafe said.

'I think he's trying to avoid Jo,' Neva confided. 'She keeps making a beeline for him and he keeps hurrying away. I don't think Gavin is a man who likes to be chased. He probably feels he's safe with Judith.'

Kyra felt sorry for Jo. She also felt a bit sorry for herself. She spent a great deal of the evening looking towards the door even though Constance had told her that Francis wasn't going to make it due to him being up in Scotland restoring a Laird's family portrait.

'He wasn't going to take the commission, especially as it was such short notice. But the Laird offered a sum that would make your eyes water, and Francis felt he had to take it. Besides, the man has contacts, and as Francis is a freelance conservator, reputation and recommendation mean a great deal.'

Kyra was even more disappointed than she thought she'd be. She wouldn't be seeing Francis this Valentine's Day, and for some reason, she had really hoped she would.

'Are you expecting someone?' Lucas asked,

just before midnight, as the door opened and Kyra's head shot round to look.

'No. I just wondered who was leaving.'

Lucas took her hand in his and smiled wanly. 'I think I am, Kyra.'

'What?' That was a surprise. 'It's unlike you to want an early night. Are you feeling OK? Do you want me to go with you?'

He shook his head and his mass of blond hair danced around his bronzed face.

'I'm fine. No. That's not true. I'm not fine. I might even be a bit heartbroken. But that's life isn't it? There's nothing we can do about it. We can't make people love us. Or stay in love with us.'

'What?' Prickles of cold ran up her arms. 'I'm not sure what you're saying, Lucas.'

'I'm saying I think we're over, don't you? It's not great timing, I guess, but hey. I didn't plan to do this tonight. Then again I didn't expect my girlfriend to spend the whole of Valentine's night looking at the door hoping someone other than me would walk in.'

Kyra swallowed hard. 'I ... I don't know what you mean.'

'Really? That's the way you're going to go? I thought we were friends above everything else, Kyra.'

'We are.'

'Then let's be honest, shall we? We owe each other that.'

She took a deep breath. 'OK, You're right. And I'll be honest. I thought I loved you, Lucas, but I don't think I do. I like you a lot. And I really want us to be friends, if we can. But I don't love you. Not in the way that Mum loves Amias. Or Uncle Rafe loves Neva. Or Uncle Adam loves Hazel. I've only realised that recently. It's not about you. It's about me.'

'Ah. That old cop out. I expected a bit better from you, Kyra. You're smart. Not quite as smart as Marcus, but not far off. He was the one who told me that you and I might not be on the same page. And I realised he was right. We talk a lot. I've been telling him all about the body in your cellar and do you know what he said?'

Kyra shook her head.

'He said that I kept mentioning Francis Raine. And I told him that it was because you kept mentioning Francis and I was just telling Marcus what you'd told me. Marcus told me I should watch my back.'

'There's nothing going on between me and Francis, Lucas. We're just friends.'

'Yeah. But you'd like to be more than friends, wouldn't you? Be honest, Kyra.'

She nodded. 'I think so. If I'm totally honest, I'm not sure how I feel.'

'I am. I think the fact that your eyes have been glued to that door says it all.'

'Oh, Lucas. I'm so sorry. I really am. I

never meant this to happen. I never wanted to hurt you.'

He shrugged. 'I know you didn't. I'll get over it. The truth is, you and I were never going to make it, were we? The only thing we have in common is our love of the sea and of water sports. And I don't blame you. There's no permanent damage. And maybe we can still hang out sometimes. Especially in the summer on the water.'

'I'd like that very much.'

'Right. I'm going to go. Unless you'd like me to walk you home?'

'No need. I'll be fine. I'll go with Gran, Mum and Amias.'

Lucas turned to walk away and suddenly turned back. 'Does he feel the same about you?'

'Who? Francis?'

Lucas smirked. 'Yes. Unless there's some other guy I don't know about.'

'No other guy. I have no idea how he feels. We laugh and joke and sometimes he flirts. But he often refers to the age difference and I think that might be a stumbling block for him.'

'I hope you work it out. See you around, Kyra.'

'Thanks, Lucas. See you around.'

She watched him walk away and smiled. She thought she might feel sad but she didn't. She was glad they could still be friends.

And she realised Lucas was right. She had

been staring at the door all night. She might as well admit it, to herself at least, if not to anyone else.

She had fallen in love with Francis Raine.

She looked around the room at all the happy couples and made herself a promise. Now that she knew how she felt, she wasn't going to wait. She wasn't going to be like her mum and love someone from afar. Or love someone and be too scared to tell them. She didn't know how Francis felt about her but there was only one way to find out.

The next time she saw Francis she would tell him how she felt. What happened after that would be up to him. If he felt the same, they could decide where to take things from there. If, on the other hand, he didn't, hopefully they could remain as friends. She wouldn't see so much of him or talk to him so often. That way madness lies, as her gran would say. No point in torturing herself by seeing someone she couldn't be with, romantically.

But it was worth the risk.

And why shouldn't she ask a man out? As she had said to everyone else, why should it always be up to the man to ask? Although that conversation had been about marriage. But it applied to dating too. Lots of women asked men on dates these days.

Maybe that's what she should do. Instead of telling him directly, how she felt, perhaps she should simply ask him out on a date. And she'd make it something romantic. She'd have to think about that.

'Where's Lucas off to?' Cat asked, coming up from behind and linking her arm through Kyra's.

'Oh! You made me jump. He's going home. And to a life without me as his girlfriend.'

'What?' Cat swung round to face Kyra. 'Have you two broken up?'

'Yep. Seems so.'

'Is this about Francis?'

'It's about two people realising they aren't in love and will be better off as friends.'

'So you'll still be friends?'

'Forever. At least I hope so.'

'Then let's go home, sweetheart. Amias says he's got to get up early in the morning.'

'Oh yes.' Kyra smiled. 'I could do with some sleep myself. I'm not used to all this excitement. The Merriment Bay Moonlight Valentine's Dance will go down in history as a night to remember. At least it will for me.'

'I think it might for Lucas, too. And now that it's over. The night, I mean. Not your relationship with Lucas. Even though that is. I almost wish I had been brave – or foolish – enough to go ahead with that damn proposal.'

'Never mind, Mum,' Kyra said, as they walked arm in arm towards the table where Amias was talking to Rafe and Adam. 'You're in love. You're together. That's all that really matters. And as for a marriage proposal, there's always tomorrow.'

Coming soon

Wedding Bells in Merriment Bay

See my website for details.

A Note from Emily

Thank you for reading this book. A little piece of my heart goes into all of my books and when I send them on their way, I really hope they bring a smile to someone's face. If this book made you smile, or gave you a few pleasant hours of relaxation, I'd love it if you would tell your friends.

I'd be really happy if you have a minute or two to post a review. Just a line will do, and a kind review makes such a difference to my day – to any author's day. Huge thanks to those of you who do so, and for your lovely comments and support on social media. Thank you.

A writer's life can be lonely at times. Sharing a virtual cup of coffee or a glass of wine, or exchanging a few friendly words on Facebook, Twitter or Instagram is so much fun.

You might like to join my Readers' Club by signing up for my newsletter. It's absolutely free, your email address is safe and won't be shared and I won't bombard you, I promise. You can enter competitions and enjoy some giveaways. In addition to that, there's my author page on Facebook and there's also a new Facebook group. You can chat with me and with other fans and get access to my book news, snippets from my daily life, early extracts from my books and lots more besides. Details are on the 'For You' page of my website. You'll find all my contact links in the Contact section following this.

I'm working on my next book right now. Let's see where my characters take us this time. Hope to chat with you soon.

To see details of my other books, please go to the books page on my website, or scan the QR code below to see all my books on Amazon.

Contact

If you want to be the first to hear Emily's news, find out about book releases, enter competitions and gain automatic entry into her Readers' Club, go to: https://www.emilyharvale.com and subscribe to her newsletter via the 'Sign me up' box. If you love Emily's books and want to chat with her and other fans, ask to join the exclusive Emily Harvale's Readers' Club Facebook group.

Or come and say 'Hello' on Facebook, Twitter and Instagram.

Contact Emily via social media:
www.twitter.com/emilyharvale
www.facebook.com/emilyharvalewriter
www.facebook.com/emilyharvale
www.instagram.com/emilyharvale

Or by email via the website:
www.emilyharvale.com

Acknowledgements

My grateful thanks go to the following:

Christina Harkness for her patience and care in editing this book.
My webmaster, David Cleworth who does so much more than website stuff.
My cover design team, JR.
Luke Brabants. Luke is a talented artist and can be found at: www.lukebrabants.com
My wonderful friends for their friendship and love. You know I love you all.
All the fabulous members of my Readers' Club. You help and support me in so many ways and I am truly grateful for your ongoing friendship. I wouldn't be where I am today without you.
My Twitter and Facebook friends, and fans of my Facebook author page. It's great to chat with you. You help to keep me (relatively) sane!
Thank you for buying this book.

Printed in Poland
by Amazon Fulfillment
Poland Sp. z o.o., Wrocław